LOVE QUEST

CAMILLA ISLEY

Boldwood

First published in 2020. This edition first publishing in Great Britain in 2023 by Boldwood Books Ltd.

Cover Design by BNP Design Studio

This book is a work of fiction and, except in the case of historical fact, any resemblance to actual persons, living or dead, is purely coincidental.

Every effort has been made to obtain the necessary permissions with reference to copyright material, both illustrative and quoted. We apologise for any omissions in this respect and will be pleased to make the appropriate acknowledgements in any future edition.

A CIP catalogue record for this book is available from the British Library.

Paperback ISBN 978-1-83751-922-4

Large Print ISBN 978-1-83751-921-7

Hardback ISBN 978-1-83751-920-0

Ebook ISBN 978-1-83751-923-1

Kindle ISBN 978-1-83751-924-8

Audio CD ISBN 978-1-83751-915-6

MP3 CD ISBN 978-1-83751-916-3

Digital audio download ISBN 978-1-83751-917-0

Boldwood Books Ltd
23 Bowerdean Street
London SW6 3TN
www.boldwoodbooks.com

To all of us who ever dreamed of going on a treasure hunt one day...

1

WINTER

"There's a naked man outside the hut next door," I say to my best friend Lana on the phone.

"Is that why we're whispering?" she asks.

"Yes."

"And why is he naked? Are you in a naturist resort?"

"Not that I know of."

"Okay, but when you say 'naked man,' are we talking elderly pal who forgot to put on his pants, or—"

"No," I interrupt her. "We're talking six foot five of prime beefcake, white butt cheeks gloriously resplendent in the morning sun."

"Uh-uh, attagirl. So, what's the stud doing in the nude? Besides providing a nice view, I mean."

I raise my gaze upward from the tush region, which so far has monopolized my attention, and take in the whole scene. "He's shouting profanities at a monkey perched on the roof of his hut."

"Why?"

I squint my eyes against the sun's glare. "The little bugger has stolen his phone. Bah, the dude should've known better."

"Hey, I don't think he volunteered the phone."

"No, but the resort is right at the edge of the jungle, and there's warning signs everywhere recommending that people keep their doors shut at all times and to beware of the monkeys. He must've forgotten to lock the door, and the little thief ran in while he was showering. Why else would he run outside naked —oh, crap!"

The man turns, and, for fear of being spotted, I squat behind my hut's bamboo railing, dropping my phone.

"Sorry," I say into the AirPods mic while retrieving the phone.

"What happened?" Lana asks.

"Dude went back inside; I had to dive for cover."

"Oh, gosh. Did you get a full frontal?"

"No, I was too quick in dropping to my knees."

"But why are you still hiding if Mr. White Cheeks is gone?"

"I don't know. He may come back."

"FaceTime me," Lana says.

"Why?"

"If you lift your phone's camera above the railing, I can tell you what's happening."

"You're a perv," I joke. "Isn't seeing the Sexiest Man Alive naked any time you want enough for you?"

My best friend is in a relationship with Hollywood's number one heartthrob—totally by accident. Fate brought them together when she needed him the most, and, while I don't envy the circumstances of their epic meet-cute, I'd be lying if I said I wasn't the teensiest bit jealous.

"Hey," Lana protests. "My interest is purely anthropological."

Out of curiosity, I do as she says, turning on the camera. Lana's face appears on the screen. I wave, smile, then flip the phone around and raise it an inch above the railing.

"What do you see?" I ask.

"Oh, shoot!"

"What?"

"He's back, but with a towel around his waist. Anyway, the bare-chest guise still has appeal." Lana sighs. "Even from a distance, I can tell he's eye candy."

"And what's the eye candy doing?"

"Talking to the monkey, I think, but he's too far away so I can't be sure."

The naked stranger's stilt villa and mine are about thirty yards apart and share a patch of grass enclosed within a square lined with hedges for privacy.

"Why don't you come out and see for yourself?" Lana suggests. "He's no longer naked."

I get up from my squatting position but stay half-hidden behind the vertical cane screen shielding the left edge of the patio. Spying between the cracks in the wood, I can make out what's happening on the other side.

"You're right," I tell Lana. "He's negotiating with the monkey."

"How does one bargain with a monkey?"

"The dude is offering a banana in exchange for his phone."

Lana chuckles. "Is the monkey taking it?"

To better peer between the gaps, I bring my face so close to the divider my nose touches the wood. "Looks like she's considering... she's extending her free hand toward the banana... and, yep, she's taken the banana and, oh, no! She's dropped the phone." I watch as the discarded piece of technology crashes to the floor, my neighbor not quick enough to catch it. "Ouch, you wouldn't believe the stream of filth that's exiting the dude's mouth. He's bending down to pick up the phone; the screen must've broken... and, oh gosh, there goes the towel... I have eyes on white butt cheeks again." I push my phone slightly out to the side so Lana can see.

"Yeah, those are some impressive buns."

We both keep an eye on the man as he takes a few quick steps to his door and, still cursing like a sailor, slams it shut.

"Aww." I sigh, turning off the video. "Show's over."

After one last peek at the monkey now enjoying her banana on the roof, I head back inside my bungalow, saying, "What's up with you?"

It's weird for Lana to call me while I'm on a work assignment out of the country.

"You have time to talk?" she asks, with an edge to her voice.

Something's definitely up.

"Not really, honey; I have a meeting with the expedition team in"—I check my watch—"twenty minutes."

"Oh, okay." She sounds downcast. "Can we talk when you come back?"

I double-check that my door is locked, then open the backpack resting against the wall next to it to get some clothes out. "Did something happen?" I ask, apprehension building in my gut.

"Yeah," Lana says. "But it's better if we talk later. You'll want to hear the whole story."

I select a pair of shorts and a loose T-shirt and lay them on the mattress. "Now I definitely want spoilers."

"Trust me, you don't."

"Do."

"Okay, but you're going to hate that you have to go to a meeting after I tell you..."

I untie the back of my bikini bra and toss it on the straw bench at the foot of the bed. "You're raising my expectations... What is it?"

"I spoke with Summer today."

Ka-Boom!

Lana drops the bomb on me.

"You're right." I sigh. "Now I don't want to hang up. But, sweetheart, I really must go. I'm already running late. I'll call you as soon as I get back, okay?"

"Sure."

"Just tell me, was it... civil?"

"Mostly, but I still don't know how to behave around your sister. That's why I called. I need to pick your brain."

"Okay, my meeting shouldn't take long; it's going to be an introduction to the expedition team and itinerary planning. I should be free in an hour tops." I make a quick calculation of the time difference between Thailand and California. In the US, it's still yesterday evening. "Or is it going to be too late in LA?"

"No, Christian is at the studio doing a voiceover. He said it'll take him hours to finish so I should be alone all night."

"All right, talk to you later."

"Later, bye."

I shimmy out of my bikini panties and walk into the stone-and-wood shower to wash off the sweat of an hour spent sunbathing on the outside patio. As I quickly foam myself up, my thoughts inevitably drift to my sister.

In the past few months, I haven't talked to her much. I still can't forgive Summer for what she did to Lana. The thought of my sister having an affair with Lana's boyfriend still sends me into a raging tailspin. But I hope that if they're mending their relationship, we, too, can find our path back to each other. Being so mad at my twin that I can't stand to see her face—incidentally, my face also—isn't healthy.

I hop out of the shower, towel off, comb my hair back without drying it, and don the clothes I prepared. Flip-flops on,

I'm ready to go. I slip out of the bungalow, opening the French windows just far enough to let me through—no monkeys in sight, but I'm not taking chances. Imagine if they stole one of my cameras... I'd be swearing far worse than Mr. White Cheeks. Yeah, better safe than sorry. Triple-checking the door is locked, I pocket the key and skip down the steps of my stilt hut to walk to the resort's reception and go meet the others.

I hope the team is solid. I've never worked with the agency that booked me for this job, so I don't know anyone on this trip.

Fingers crossed.

Nothing could be worse than being stuck in the jungle for three weeks with a bunch of morons.

* * *

Logan

I stare at my watch impatiently. Everyone's here, except for the photographer.

When the Social Sciences dean told me a woman had been hired, I tried to persuade him to cancel. But Dr. Voss insisted she came highly recommended, and I couldn't make a fuss. Securing the funding to finance this entire operation has already been close to impossible, and since UC Berkeley is our sole sponsor, I wasn't able to put my foot down too hard.

But now I wish I had.

Bringing a woman on board was a terrible idea. I've nothing against women per se. My ex and I went on countless archeological trips together. But a few bad experiences with mixed-gender teams afterward have taught me what a nightmare having to deal with relationship drama on an expedition can be. I never want to go through that again. And this trip will be no joke; with weeks of heavy trekking ahead, it'll be physically exhausting even for the most trained of us, and I'm used to setting a punishing pace. No matter how fit the photographer is, she's bound to slow the group down. Plus, having one woman join a team of eight men is going to be an unwanted distraction on its own. We won't even be able to take a leak without making a fuss.

I hope she's at least ugly. Or married. Less chance of my team falling over themselves trying to impress her if she is. I have enough problems without adding yet another to the mix.

Already this expedition hasn't started in the best of ways. I unlock and re-lock my phone, reading the time on the newly-cracked screen. Fifteen minutes late and counting. I can already tell she's going to be a massive headache for me.

I snort and walk to the refreshment table to grab another pineapple juice. The humidity in this place is overwhelming. Even standing in the shade of the Welcome Center—an open-walled wooden structure with a thatched roof—there's no break from the heat.

I pick up a glass covered in condensation and turn back to re-join the others, almost choking on my first sip when I spot a slender blonde walking into the hotel's reception.

Her wet platinum-gold hair frames an angelic face—big blue eyes, rosy cheeks, and full lips. And the body that goes with the face... Well, let's just say it brings to mind a very different kind of angel, as in, the ones walking down the runway at the annual Victoria's Secret Fashion Show—generous rack, tiny waist, legs that never seem to end.

The blonde is wearing a flimsy T-shirt and a pair of light-washed jean shorts that are basically underwear. Really, she has great legs. I low whistle in my head, thinking the wait and the heat suddenly aren't quite as annoying with this gorgeous woman to distract me.

My appreciation turns to dismay as the blonde takes a quick scan of the reception, pinpoints our group, and promptly walks toward the team to introduce herself, shaking hands left and right. It would appear our photographer has arrived.

I gape at the scene, aghast, as a band of hardened men transforms into a pack of doting puppies all wagging their metaphorical tails.

Please tell me this isn't happening.

Oh, but it is.

All my worries are confirmed when I study the group's dynamic now that a pin-up has joined the ranks. She's the focus of everyone's attention, all the sensible topics my colleagues were discussing beforehand forgotten at once. How are we going to get anything done?

The only attitude worse than the widespread adoration is the approving leer curving the lips of Colonel Smith, our chief of security and another member of my team I didn't pick.

I wasn't eager for a squadron of mercenaries to join the expedition in the first place. But Smith and his two minions are one more nuisance that came as a package deal with the funding. I can't help not liking the man; he honestly gives me the creeps. An ex-Delta Force assault squad leader, Smith has turned to private security in his retirement. Of an undecipherable age somewhere between forty-five and fifty-five, he's retained all his military bearing: buzz cut, lean muscled body, and a hard face marked by a livid white slash. The ominous scar cuts from his left eyebrow to halfway down his cheek. And he probably enjoys frightening children with it in his spare time.

The colonel is dressed in a military-like uniform of all black —from shirt, to boots, to weapons—and he looks like he's constantly standing at attention. And so do the other two soldiers, Carter and Montgomery—all three men only provided surnames—who also are ex-Special Forces. The trio is inseparable, apparently.

I drop the empty juice glass on the appropriate tray and join the rest of the team, ready to tighten the leash before my puppies get in a dog fight to gain the photographer's attention.

"This should be everyone," I say, entering the semicircle the others have formed. "Why don't we make the introductions official? I'm Dr. Logan Spencer."

The woman turns toward me, her eyes widening as if in... recognition? Nah, impossible. I'm sure we haven't met; I'd remember a face like that. Next, she blushes slightly, and, finally, her expression settles on a half-amused grin she's working hard to suppress. What does she have to smirk about? It's unnerving.

Determined not to get sidetracked by the woman's cryptic half-smile—See? She's already a distraction—I tear my eyes away from the blonde and continue with my self-introduction. "I'm the lead archeologist on this team, and also a professor of Archeological Research Strategy at Berkeley University. Before I lay out the details of our itinerary, I thought it'd be good for each team member to introduce himself to—"

"Or herself," the woman interrupts.

Oh, great, so the killer looks come paired with a feisty personality. Looks like I've won the Pain-In-My-Ass Photographer lottery.

"Sure." I nod toward her, trying to keep the annoyance from showing on my face. "And tell everyone his or her role." I tilt my head in her direction. "Ladies first?"

She flashes me an impertinent grin, and says, "Winter Knowles, travel photographer."

That seems like all she has to say. Miss Knowles, at least, is not overly talkative. Without adding another word, she turns to the guy standing on her left, none other than my best friend, Archie, who quickly takes the prompt.

"Archibald—Archie—Hill," he says, with a grin that promises nothing good. I know him too well; he's already trying to impress the lady. Tall, blond, bearded, and with piercing blue eyes, he usually doesn't have to try too hard in that department. "Topographer, aerial drone controller, and human bullshit detector."

Winter laughs, a light and bubbly sound. "We have a drone?" she asks with a big smile.

"Yup," Archie confirms, smug.

"You'll have to show me how to handle it."

He grins. "I'm sure we can make that happen."

Then my best friend and trusted companion of many past expeditions turns away from Winter and wiggles his eyebrows at me, as if saying he'd be more than happy to teach her how to handle it. I resist the urge to slap my hand over my face and groan.

This is a disaster.

Eager to move on, I stare at the next guy in our circle until he takes the hint.

"Dr. Rune Boonjan," the short man says in heavily accented English. "Head archeologist at the Thai Fine Arts Department, local expert, and interpreter."

Dr. Boonjan and I met in person for the first time on the plane from Bangkok to Trat, and he impressed me with his knowledge of the history of the Kingdom of Siam. No worries about him; we clicked right away.

Dr. Boonjan bends in a slight bow, his palms pressed together in a prayer-like fashion, and salutes us in Thai, "*Sawatdee khrap.*"

We all bow back, mimicking his salutation except for the military guys, who remain upright.

Rude.

Then, the group's focus shifts to the other Thai member of our team. About the same height as Dr. Boonjan, he's leaner, and his brown skin looks more weathered even though he's younger.

"Somchai Inkong," he introduces, in English even more accented than the professor's, making it a task in concentration to understand him. "Horses and mules handler, local fixer, and"—he gives a cheeky grin—"machete operator. *Sawatdee khrap.*"

"*Sawatdee khrap,*" we repeat.

I turn to my right to encourage Tucker to speak—he's the only other known factor in this group besides myself and Archie. He hasn't been with us from the start, but since our first trip together in Guatemala, he has become an invaluable member of every new expedition Archie and I plan.

"Tucker Wallace," he announces in his clear baritone voice. "Logistics, cooking, and first aid."

"We have a cook?" Winter says. "Yay! I'd assumed we would eat beef jerky for a month." She smiles at Tucker, probably more pleased at the thought of his cooking skills than anything else, but there he goes turning into an adoring puppy like the rest of them.

Not him, too!

Women are Archie's weakness, but Tucker is usually smarter than that. With brown eyes and a mop of curly brown hair, he's the shy, responsible guy in our group. The teddy bear looks don't fool anyone for long, though; when it comes to his job, Tucker is a dictator with an iron fist.

The next man in our circle, at least, has no puppy in him. Although I'm not sure "hungry wolf" is much better. I'll have to keep an eye on him and his pack when they're around Winter. Because I didn't have enough to do already.

"Smith," the mercenary says, not shifting an inch from his military resting pose—feet hip-width apart, puffed out chest, hands clasped behind his back. "Head of security."

His two deputies echo him, keeping the same stance and not providing any additional personal details.

"Carter."

"Montgomery."

These military guys are so full of themselves, they're ridiculous. And I can tell from the mocking twinkle in Winter's eyes that she's thinking along the same lines. She bites her lower lip as if she's having to physically stop herself from uttering whatever barb she's thinking.

Definitely distracting.

"All right, that was everyone," I say, ready to wrap up the meeting. "I'm sure we'll have plenty of time to become more familiar with each other in the upcoming weeks." Archie throws me a rakish, I-plan-to-get-oh-so-familiar-with-our-photographer look. I pause to scowl at him, then add, "Tomorrow we leave at the crack of dawn. Before you go enjoy your last day in the comforts of civilization, I'll ask Tucker to walk us through the logistics of our first stretch on the road."

"Great." Tucker takes out his rugged tablet and shows the group a map on the screen. "The first part of tomorrow's journey will be on the Jeeps." He traces the path on the map with his finger. "Our destination isn't far from the resort, but the road to get there is more of an abandoned dirt trail winding up the mountains." He points to the three peaks on our left. "Halfway up, we'll stop at the only village inland to collect our last few provisions. From there, we'll continue the crossing on horseback while the mules will carry most of the equipment and supplies. If everything goes according to plan, we should reach our final destination, the hidden valley beyond the peaks, before the sun sets. Once there, we'll build our base of operations and proceed with our exploration on foot over the next days with the support of our local bush-whacking guide."

Tucker nods at Somchai, who returns the gesture with a grin.

"Anyway," Tucker continues, "we meet in the parking lot tomorrow at 5 a.m., so we should all get an early night."

He steps back, and I take the floor again.

"I'm sure there's no need to point this out," I say, staring directly at the photographer. "But we're going to be traveling through a hostile environment, so we should all dress appropriately. And," I add, "punctuality is of the essence."

Winter bites her lip again, but doesn't comment. Even if the hard stare she's giving me promises hell.

Before I dismiss the meeting, I deliver one last warning. "And finally, just a reminder that the nature of this expedition is confidential. If someone asks, our cover story is that we're in Thailand to study the ecology of the region. Flora, fauna, rock formations... that kind of stuff. So, please, no loose talk about a lost city of gold. See you all at five tomorrow," I conclude.

After my dismissal, the group breaks apart. The military guys leave, marching away in single file. The two locals speak among themselves in thick Thai and then walk off in the opposite direction. Archie and Tucker join me to go over the last details of tomorrow's journey.

I hope the photographer will head back to her bungalow without any further demonstration of her saucy attitude.

"Excuse me?"

No such luck. I've just started talking to Archie when she materializes behind my back, demanding attention.

"Yes?" I say, turning to her. Archie stands on my left, Tucker on my right.

I tower a good few inches over her, but the photographer doesn't appear one bit intimidated as she asks, "Do you have a problem with me?"

Busted.

"Is it because I have tits?"

As she says the words, three sets of eyes lower to her chest.

When I raise my gaze again to meet hers, she's giving me a hand-on-the-hip, have-you-had-enough-of-a-good-look, sarcastic pout.

Well, she can't speak that word in front of three men and expect any other reaction. It was practically a directive to look.

"Because I can assure you, I'm a professional." Flaring up with self-righteous indignation, Miss Sass continues her tirade, "Not my first drill, you know?"

"Sure," I say, dutifully chastised. "Sorry if I appeared disrespectful."

"You didn't choose me for this job, did you?"

No point in lying. "No."

"Didn't want a woman on board?"

"Nothing personal."

"No, of course. Well, no need to worry. I can pull my weight and take care of myself. No damsels in distress here."

Then she stops for a second, looking undecided whether she should go on with whatever she's dying to say next.

She goes for it. "Like, for instance, I can read and comprehend the million warning signs around me."

What the hell is she talking about?

With an evil little smirk playing on her lips, she asks, "How's that broken phone treating you?"

I blink at her.

How can she possibly know?

The grin widens, and she answers the question I haven't asked.

"Our bungalows are adjoining," she explains. "Next time, I'd suggest doing as the signs say and locking your doors." Then, with a wink, she adds, "Nice negotiating skills, by the way. I'm sure they'll come in handy in the jungle."

My face flames red hot, and I can only hope I'm not blushing like a schoolgirl.

I don't have to look at them to know that both Archie and Tucker are tremendously enjoying me being told off. Usually, I'm the one doing the scolding.

Winter nods at them, saying, "Gentlemen," and then walks away, leaving us to admire her long legs as she saunters down the road.

As soon as she rounds the corner, Archie low whistles. "Imagine how that feistiness translates in bed!"

And damn me, because my friend's words conjure up all kinds of wrong fantasies.

"Dude?" Tucker asks. "What was she talking about with keeping the doors locked?"

And, as if my humiliation wasn't complete enough, now I have to explain to my friends about my earlier disagreement with the local fauna...

2

WINTER

The second I get back to my bungalow, I call Lana.

"You're never going to believe this," I say the instant my best friend picks up.

"What?" Lana asks, a hint of playful curiosity in her voice.

"Guess who the esteemed expedition leader, who incidentally hates women, is?"

"Who?"

"Mr. White Cheeks," I say, collapsing onto the bed.

"I take it the introductions didn't go well?" she asks, now definitely amused. Easy for her to laugh; she doesn't have to spend the next month trekking through the Thai jungle with Satan. "And how come he hates women?"

I sigh. "Maybe 'hate' is a strong word." I rest my back against the headboard and tuck my knees close to my chest. "It was more the attitude sailors used to have about women onboard ships."

"And what was that?"

"That we're bad luck or something. What an insufferable, dumb snob."

"If he's leading such an important expedition, he can't be that stupid. Didn't you say you're after a legendary lost city?"

My heart does a little guilty flip, Satan's words ringing in my ears. *The nature of this expedition is confidential... No loose talk about a lost city of gold.*

The dude's so paranoid he even made everyone sign NDAs about it. An agreement I might have broken already by telling Lana... But I honestly don't see what the big deal is with all this secrecy, and Lana's my best friend, so she doesn't count.

"I'm not supposed to talk about that," I say, deflecting Lana's question. And trust me, he can be that dumb."

"Mm." Lana says nothing, but still sounds as if she's enjoying herself.

"You don't seem sympathetic."

"No, sorry. It's just that I haven't heard you so worked up about someone, well... ever."

"I know! He's the most annoying, arrogant bastard—"

"Does he have a name?" Lana interrupts.

"Logan."

"Kind of a sexy name to go with a sexy ass."

"Oh, pfft, please. I take back everything nice I ever said about his anatomy. He doesn't deserve it. And from now on, we're referring to him as Satan."

"How's the face that goes with the ass?" Lana asks. "I couldn't see over the phone; is he ugly?"

"He's a type," I say neutrally.

"What type?"

"Thick brown hair, hazel-green eyes, full lips, slight chin cleft, a few freckles..."

"Sounds like everyone's type."

I scoff. "If you enjoy watching a constant scowl. And, anyway, it doesn't matter if he's not repellent, physically, he's still evil inside. Most beautiful things in nature are. Like, you wouldn't kiss a cobra or eat a moonflower."

"So kissing Satan would never cross your mind?"

"Haven't you been listening? Of course it wouldn't."

"I have been paying attention, that's why I'm asking. You're the one who brought up kissing, not me."

"You don't get it!"

"What? That your boss—so to speak—is tall, handsome... presumably smart—"

"And arrogant, and full of himself, definitely evil, and I hate his guts."

"Whoa, he really crossed you, considering you only spent, what, an hour with him?"

"You should've seen him." I use my mocking voice again. "'We should all dress appropriately for the jungle,' as if he expected me to show up in a skirt and heels."

"Guess Logan is not used to having a bombshell as a member of his team."

"Satan," I correct her. "And bombshell, me? That's Summer. I'm the tomboy."

"You're identical twins, who share 99.99 per cent of your DNA."

"Still, we couldn't be more different. Speaking of evil twins... Sorry for monopolizing the conversation, but I needed to vent."

"No worries."

"So, Summer." I go back to the topic Lana meant to discuss earlier. "Tell me everything. Did you speak with her in person?"

"Yeah, she called, asked if I wanted to grab a coffee and talk."

"You're a much bigger person than I am; if I'd caught her screwing my boyfriend I'd never talk to her again, even if she's my sister."

"You still sound angrier than I am," Lana notes.

"I told you, you're the better person. Plus, you have the Sexiest Man Alive to distract you as a consequence of what Summer pulled. I don't."

Lana chuckles. "Ah, you have a point. Without Christian in my life, I wouldn't be so Zen about everything. But, you're right, Summer's actions resulted in me being the happiest I've ever been, while she... your sister isn't in good shape, to be honest."

Some deep, ancestral bond makes my insides twinge with worry. Summer might be the evil twin, but she's my evil twin.

"How bad?" I ask.

"Nothing obvious on the outside, but it's like she's had her spirit broken. She was a ghost of her former self. Promise you'll go see her when you come back. If I can forgive her, you should, too."

"You forgave her?"

"As much as I know how. Our friendship won't ever be the same as before, but I saw no point in holding a grudge forever..."

"Doesn't the fact that she's in a relationship with your ex bother you?"

"She and John broke up."

"What?" I say, straightening up. This is huge. "How? When?"

"After he sold the story to the press, his sorry version of it. She cut him loose after reading the feature."

"But that was a month ago!"

"You haven't talked to her in that long?"

"No," I admit, guilt gnawing at my insides. Before now, Summer and I had never had a fight that lasted this long. "It's been easier not to call her since I've been away."

The new job starts tomorrow, but I've spent the past four weeks in Bangkok on another assignment.

"Anyway," Lana continues. "Summer told me she was completely blindsided by the magazine piece. John didn't tell her before going to the press, and she felt like he'd sold her dignity for 10,000 dollars. He didn't consider for a second what the article would do to her, to her reputation... She also said she hated the way he spoke about me—'revolting,' to quote her."

"Well..." I relax my back against the pillows again. "'Cause he's a disgusting piece of shit."

"I guess."

"My sister threw away a lifetime of friendship for a three-month affair. I still can't wrap my head around it."

"She had broken up with Robert only a few months before. Maybe the separation hit her harder than we thought."

"How can you make justifications for her?"

Lana lets a few seconds pass before answering. "I thought seeing her at rock bottom would give me satisfaction, but it really didn't. Honestly, I'm gutted for her, but I can't be there to help her, I don't have it in me, not yet. I just wish you were here. How much longer are you gone for?"

Again, guilt kicks around in my guts. "A few weeks at least, possibly more. Why do you think she reached out to you today? Why wait a month after she broke up with Johnathan?"

"She read the *Vanity Fair* feature about Christian and me being back together. She thought I'd be more willing to hear her out since I was so happy."

"Which I guess you were."

"Yup. Speaking of..." Lana pauses. "Christian just got back in."

"I'll let you go, then."

"Will you be reachable over the next few days?"

"Afraid not, we're moving inland tomorrow, no service there."

"Please call Summer today, then, before you go off the grid."

"You're really an angel."

"Am not. And you'd do the same if it were me. Remember

when I kissed Peter Gomez in the locker room and Summer didn't talk to me for a week? You were there to advocate for me."

"That was the eleventh grade."

"It doesn't matter. Promise you'll call your sister."

"Okay, I promise. Love you."

"Love you."

We hang up, and I remain motionless on the bed looking at my phone for the longest time.

Why am I being so stubborn? Why am I still so mad at Summer? If Lana can forgive her, I should be able to as well.

Maybe I shouldn't ask myself to make peace with my twin all at once.

Right!

Baby steps.

I unlock my phone and tap her contact before I can change my mind.

Summer picks up after five long rings.

"Hello?"

Her voice sounds broken, as if she... "Are you crying?"

"A little," she says. "But nothing serious. I'm just watching *Notting Hill*, the bit where Julia Roberts goes back to the shop and tells Hugh Grant she's just a girl..."

My sister getting sentimental over romantic comedies? Lana was right, the situation is major.

"Where are you?" Summer asks. "The line sounds weird."

"Thailand, near the coast. But I'm leaving for the jungle tomorrow. Thought I'd give you a call, as I won't have service for a few weeks."

Summer instantly calls bullshit on my story. "Lana told you to check in on me, didn't she?"

"She did," I admit.

"Guess you're up to date on all the big news, then."

"I am, and to be honest, I'm glad you've broken up with Johnathan. He's a cockroach who never deserved you or Lana."

"True. Which only makes me feel worse..." Her voice cracks again.

I swallow back all the harsh retorts that pop into my head and try to be conciliatory.

"At least now it's over," I say.

I'm not being the most uplifting, but... I'm trying.

"Can we... not talk about any of that, please?" Summer pleads. "Tell me about your trip. How's the team? Mom's worried because you've never worked with any of them before..."

That's all the encouragement I need to tell my sister how I ended up working for Satan.

"He sounds like a handful," Summer chuckles when I'm done. And that deep part of me that is linked to her for life whoops with joy that I could cheer her up a little. "How about the rest of the team? Anyone interesting?"

"Bah, the security team guys are all buffs, but they take themselves too seriously. The only fascinating fella is the topographer."

"Fascinating how?"

"Think tall Viking warrior with dirty-blond hair and ice-blue eyes that stand out against his tan skin. Oh, and did I mention? The man has a beard."

"Ew. I hate beards."

"Just because you've never kissed one; his looks like the soft type."

"Well, enjoy your bearded Viking." Summer yawns. "I'll let Mom know your team is cool."

Leader aside, I think, but only say, "Thanks."

"No problem."

I have no response, and she doesn't say anything else.

Suddenly our easy flow of conversation is gone, and things become super awkward again.

After a few seconds, Summer yawns again, a bit too loudly to be genuine. "Well, the movie's over, and I have to go if I want to wake up at a decent hour tomorrow..."

"Yeah, right. Of course."

"Thanks for calling."

For a few brief, wonderful minutes, we've been the Knowles twins again, inseparable from birth. But now we're back to walking on eggshells around each other. I still haven't forgiven Summer for what she did, and she knows it. A conversation, no matter how nice, isn't enough to mend our relationship.

But, as I said: baby steps.

"Sure," I say. "I'll let you get to sleep. Night."

"Night."

When the line goes dead, I drop the phone on the nightstand and lay on the bed, staring at the ceiling.

Lana was right: holding a grudge is no good. Now that I've talked to Summer, I feel a million times better, at least mentally.

Physically, I'm about to melt. The room has gotten too hot; the air conditioning is crap and does nothing against the midday Thai heat. Good thing there's an ocean just a few yards away. I change back into my bikini and go for a swim.

* * *

Logan

"Man," I say to Archie, snapping my fingers. "I'm talking to you."

Archie, Tucker and I are seated outside at a table in the

shade under the giant wooden hut where the resort serves breakfast and lunch. We're discussing more in detail the laser-scanned images of the area we are to explore on foot and the difficulties we might encounter reaching it. But it seems I'm the only person interested in the topic. My two friends are staring behind my shoulders like two hypnotized dummies.

"Sorry." Archie's ice-blue eyes flicker to me. "I was enjoying the view."

A twitch of his mustached upper lip lets me know he's not talking about the ocean.

I turn toward the beach just in time to see Miss Pain-in-my-ass Knowles walk out of the sea with the same sex appeal as a Bond girl in a *007* movie: wet hair swept back, water dripping down her body, wearing a bikini so skimpy it makes the shorts she had on before look like nun-ware.

If that wasn't enough, she walks straight to the beach shower.

"Tucker," Archie says. "Please tell me there's going to be open showers at our camp."

I turn back and find both of them still staring like imbeciles.

"No," Tucker says. "But if we ration drinking water we could make one just for her."

"I'm ready to die a happy, thirsty man," Archie replies without removing his eyes from the photographer.

See? See? That's why I didn't want a woman on board. It's objectively disrupting. And a woman like that...

I throw another furtive stare behind my shoulder just as Winter closes the water faucet and walks back to the beach to go lie down on a chaise lounge by the shore, finally out of sight.

"Okay," I say. "Now that the show's over, can we please concentrate?"

"You should learn how to appreciate the small joys of life,

Logie Bear," Archie says, using my college-football-playing-days nickname.

"A groundbreaking discovery of an ancient, untouched city is what would give me joy." I flare my nostrils and point at the open maps on the table. "You were saying we won't have a clear path of approach?"

Archie throws me another don't-be-such-a-spoilsport look before he continues. "What these images tell us is that beyond this position"—he points at the red-circled area Tucker has selected as our base camp—"we will have to hack our way through every inch of jungle to reach across"—he moves his finger to the other red circle on the map identifying our destination, code-named Area X—"to here. It's a jungle stretch just shy of fifteen miles that will take us at least seven or eight days to clear."

"Tucker," I say. "What is your suggested approach? Should we advance each day, leaving enough time to circle back to the main camp, or should we set up secondary, one-night-only camps as we go? I'd prefer this second solution; it'd save us time."

"I'd rather circle back to base, at least for the first few days. Unless you want to get eaten by a tiger, that is." He stares down at the aerial pictures, where only thick green vegetation is visible. If it weren't for the correlated laser scans, no one could've guessed the jungle harbors more than just vines and trees. "The place we're going is so wild, the animals there must've never seen a man."

"That's why we hired a security team. I'm sure they can scare off a few big cats," I counter. "Those military guys don't look like they're joking around."

Archie scoffs sarcastically. "Aye, aye."

"Still," Tucker says. "We have no idea what's waiting for us out there, and I'd rather we all got back in one piece. It's not an everyday thing to reach one of the last unexplored regions on Earth."

Archie pulls at his short beard. "Let's hope we actually find something when we get to Area X."

We have to. I've put everything on the line to organize this trip. My career, my reputation... I can't fail.

The legend of a lost city made of gold and hidden in the thick of the Thai jungle has haunted me since I first heard it the summer of my freshman year in college, when I spent a month backpacking in this country. Since then, finding the legendary city has become an obsession of mine. I've spent years collecting every scrap of research I could find on the topic.

But the area the various rumors pointed at had always been too vast to grant any real hope of success. Until I heard of a new technology that could take an aerial scan of even the thickest forest and reveal what lay hidden underneath. A city.

But will it truly be the legend I've spent years tracking and obsessing over?

3

WINTER

When I get back to my villa from the beach, it's already dark outside. One minute the sun was up, and the next it had disappeared behind the mountains.

Inside the hut, the AC is still doing a crap job, and the atmosphere is suffocating. I wish I could leave the French windows open to let the evening breeze in. But, as per the thieving monkey population, I'd better not. Still, I need the fresh air, so I jump on the bed and examine the overhead window.

Bingo!

There's a fixed mosquito screen, unlike the sliding one that protects the door. It should be safe to leave this window open...

Mmm... I sigh in relief as a gust of fresh night air blows in my face. Then, I hop off the bed and move to the bathroom to take my last—for how long?—hot shower.

I stay under the water as long as I can, enjoying this simple comfort of civilization. But when the heat makes me light-headed, I have no choice but to step out. I wrap myself in a towel and collapse on the bed to lie down for a minute.

"...Nah, man, come on." Logan's voice drifts in from the open window.

Hey, I said I wanted to relax, not listen to Satan yapping. I'm tempted to get up and close the window, but the night air feels too good on my wet skin. And I'm just too plain lazy to move right now.

"We have to," Archibald the Viking replies. "It's a tradition."

"Shouldn't we wait until after dinner?"

"No, Tucker wants everyone to go straight to bed, and we can't rush this. You have glasses?"

"Inside," Logan says, sounding resigned. "And close the door," he adds.

I smirk to myself. Looks like Satan is a quick study.

There's a moment of silence, followed by the sound of the sliding door opening and closing, a few quiet minutes, and finally the door again.

Then Archie speaks.

"Here's a glass of the best bourbon money can't buy."

"Amazing, man. Priscilla still sends you a bottle every year?"

Archie's reply is jokingly cocky. "Must've made quite an impression on the lady, haven't I?"

"That you did," Logan agrees in a tone of friendly reproach.

"To a new adventure," Archie declares. "And the greatest archeological discovery of the millennium."

"Cheers."

They clink glasses and presumably drink. There's another pause before Logan talks again.

"Speaking of ladies," he says. "I call dibs on the photographer."

"What?" Archie bursts out.

What? I echo in my head. I thought the professor hated my guts.

"Seemed like you weren't interested," Archie says. "And since when do you mix business and pleasure?"

"I don't," Logan replies, sounding infuriatingly complacent.

"So why...? Wait a minute!" Archie protests, riled up. "You can't call dibs on her just to cockblock me."

"I can, and I did."

Oh, Satan thinks he's so smug.

I, on the contrary, am not pleased with either man. The nerve of them to barter between themselves over who should "get the girl." Well, sorry guys, I'm not some brainless object you can trade amongst yourselves.

Both gentlemen would greatly benefit from a meal of humble pie.

"Dude." There's a mocking note in Archie's voice. "Are you sure the dibs has nothing to do with the lady having the best pair of legs I've ever seen, not to mention pretty big..."

He doesn't finish the phrase, only makes a caveman noise. But I know he's not talking about my big eyes. I can practically see Archie mimicking cupping boobs.

"She's a beautiful woman," Logan says. A compliment that, coming from Satan's lips, doesn't resonate as one. It's like Logan has to admit I'm attractive against his will, and he resents me for it. And his next sentence confirms I'm right. "There's no denying it. But she's been a giant pain in my ass from the moment I set eyes on her." Why? What did I do, besides existing and being female, I mean? "So, yes, I'm sure."

"If you say so." Archie sounds unconvinced.

"Promise me you won't try to get in her panties," Logan insists. "This expedition is important to me, Arch. I need you to be focused. Promise me."

"All right, man, I swear. Relax..."

"When you and the genteel sex are involved, I can't. I'm only trying to avoid another Acapulco."

"Ah, yes, that would be impractical."

"Impractical? You nearly got us both killed. The lady's father chased us off his property with a loaded shotgun."

These two sound like they have a lot of history together.

"Okay," Archie concedes. "You've made your point. But—"

"No buts!"

"—if the lady can't resist me and tries something, I can't make assurances..."

"You're incorrigible! Sooner or later it'll come back to bite you in the ass."

"Until then."

I hear the clinking of ice in a glass, as if Archie just raised his drink in a mock toast.

There's a pause, and then Archie talks again. "You worry too much, my friend. You said it yourself: the scans don't lie. Something man-built lies hidden in this jungle."

"But is it the legendary lost city of gold?"

"Would it make any difference if it were only stone?"

"No," Logan admits. "It'd still be the greatest discovery of the century."

"Even greater than an untouched pharaoh tomb?" Archie asks, an edge to his voice.

"Low blow, man," Logan says, sounding displeased. "She has nothing to do with this."

She? There's a she?

Archie sighs. "Too soon?"

"Can we please not talk about women ever again?"

"And where would the fun be in that?" After a few moments of silence, Archie continues, "Let's make a bet instead. How long do you reckon before the photographer falls at my feet?"

I'm tempted to jump on the bed and yell, "Not gonna happen!" out of the window, but I keep my anger in check. Vengeance is a plate better served cold. And both gentlemen definitely need to be taken down a peg or two.

But how?

Archie is an easy fix. Ignore his sex appeal, show him I'm immune to his charms, and his ego will get bruised all right.

But what about Satan?

Dr. McEvil seems like someone who hates to make mistakes. Which means all I have to do is prove he's wrong about me. But first, I might need to bait him a little more.

Oh, the two of them, they think they're so hot and clever. But wait until they meet the real me. They won't know what hit them.

Boys, beware... Winter is coming!

4

WINTER

"Time to go eat," Archie says a while later.

The two smartasses are still out there on Logan's patio, drinking, and effectively trapping me inside my hut. I don't feel like going out as long as they're there.

"And?" Logan asks.

"The whole team is getting together; someone should invite Miss Knowles."

Silence.

"Either you go, or I do," Archie continues. "I'm sure she'd rather see my handsome face than your ugly snout."

Logan scoffs.

"Come on, man, work with me, you're being completely irrational," Archie says. "The lady has rubbed you the wrong way only because she's beautiful and because she gave you a verbal ass-kicking you totally deserved."

Okay, Mr. Hill, you're already walking up redemption road; maybe I should go easy on you.

Logan doesn't reply.

"Dude," Archie says, humor fading from his tone. "We are a

team, and you're the leader. You can't push a member out just because you don't like her. Time to grow a pair, buddy."

And the Viking continues to impress. He's not all swag and muscles. You know what? I'm taking back my decision to mess with him. He's officially off my hit list.

"All right," Logan snaps. "I'll invite her. Happy?"

Satan makes asking me to dinner sound like such a chore.

"Use some of your good-boy charm while you're at it," Archie quips, "won't you?"

Wait, so Logan is supposed to be the good one of the pair?

Ah.

And charm? What charm? If the man had any charm, it'd work on the monkeys at best! And not even. He had to bribe the macaque with a banana.

"You think she's in her bungalow?" Logan asks.

"Yep, and she's most likely been listening to every word we've said, silently hating us."

Aha. If only you knew, my sweet Viking.

"Nah," Logan says. "If she had been, she would've already come out to kick my butt and yours."

I love how Satan sounds so cocksure while being so utterly wrong.

"All right, buddy." A chair scrapes, signaling Archie getting up. "I'll see you at the restaurant."

I listen to the Viking's steps as he walks away. Then it hits me that Satan is on his way over, and I'm lying on my bed in a towel.

How much time do I have?

Should I pretend I'm only now getting out of the shower?

No, I don't want him to see me half-naked.

So what should I wear?

A mean idea takes form in my head. I smile to myself as I eye the closed suitcase of "city clothes" I'd packed for my stay in

Bangkok, and that I plan to deposit at the hotel's reception tomorrow since I won't be needing them in the jungle.

My only regret is that I didn't bring heels.

* * *

Logan

Armed with plenty of patience, I walk up the steps of my neighbor's hut, ready to get another good dose of sass.

I try to put myself in a positive headspace. Maybe Archie is right, and the sass is just her way of being defensive. Maybe she won't hinder the mission after all. I should give her the benefit of the doubt. And, as the expedition leader, it is my duty to make sure the team is united.

So, with the proverbial hat in my hands, I step on her patio and ring the hut's bell.

"I'm coming," Winter calls from the other side. "Just a second."

I respectfully wait a few steps back from the door.

Scuffling noises fill the inside of the hut, until Winter slides the French doors open. All of a sudden, she's not my annoying team member anymore, but instead that bombshell who took my breath away before I realized who she was. And she's doing it again now; it feels like she's knocked the air right out of my lungs.

Tonight, she's decided to torture me with a halter neck black dress that clings to her body like sin, following each generous curve as though a tailor designed it specifically for her. Her hair hangs in soft waves reaching to her waist. Black gladiator sandals wind up her toned legs, stopping just before the dress starts.

And I don't know why, but all those tiny leather straps around her calves are distressing.

"What can I do for you, Dr. Spencer?" Winter asks, a definite note of sarcasm audible in her tone.

I snap out of my daze and meet her eyes; a challenge awaits me there. As if she's daring me to criticize her attire choice. Did she wear this on purpose, to provoke me? Or is this just her wardrobe, what she's planning to wear on the expedition?

I take a deep breath, remembering what Archie said. I'm the team leader, and I need to be the bigger person. If the photographer wants to trek through the jungle wearing a skirt, she can be my guest, and find out the hard way why that's a terrible idea. It's not my job to tell her how to live her life. Heck, she can come in heels for all I care. And when she breaks a leg, Archie can carry her the rest of the way, and they can be happy together.

So, no, sorry, Miss Sass, not taking the bait.

"We got off on the wrong foot," I say, and only receive back an even more sarcastic, "you think?" stare. I don't let it frazzle me as I continue, "I wanted to apologize if I came off as unwelcoming earlier."

The impossible woman says nothing; she just stares at me with an "aaand?" attitude. Is she serious? That was a perfectly respectable apology! Guess I'm not done groveling. Talk about high maintenance!

"You're a valued member of this team," I go on. "And I can't wait to see you at work. I'm told you're the best in your field."

Finally, she cracks the tiniest satisfied smile and gives me an almost imperceptible nod.

"Okay, Dr. Spencer." She flips her hair back in an exaggerated motion that pushes out her chest. I have to concentrate hard not to shift my gaze to her cleavage. How is everything... staying in place like that? I don't see any bra straps. "You get the benefit of the doubt," she says, and, regarding me with a penetrating stare, she adds, "Anything else troubling you?"

And she's successfully made me blush for the second time in a day. But she can't possibly know I'm thinking about her bra, or lack thereof. Or maybe she can. Standing with her chest pushed out like that can't be natural. Is she messing with me?

"Well?" she prompts.

"No," I say quickly. "I mean, yes!" Damn, I'm making a fool of myself. Not a good look for the expedition leader. "The team is getting together for a casual dinner at the resort's restaurant. I was wondering if you'd like to join us? I, err, would be really pleased if you did."

I swear, asking my first girlfriend out in high school as an inexperienced teenage boy was easier than this.

"Sure," Miss Sass says. "Hang on a second."

She backtracks inside her bungalow, pointedly closing the door, and comes back two minutes later with a black camera strapped around her neck and nestled squarely between her—

"See something you like, Dr. Spencer?"

"That's a nice camera," I babble. "How many megapixels?"

Did I seriously just ask about the resolution of her reflex?

"No pixels for this baby." She smirks condescendingly. "Only old-fashioned film. And before you say anything, don't worry, the expedition reportage will all be in modern high-res digital shots. This is for me." She taps the camera. "I want to take a few photographs of the ocean at night."

Is that even possible? I wonder. With no light? But I don't ask, I only nod.

She gestures at the steps. "After you, Dr. Spencer."

I'm sure the use of my academic title is a form of mocking for her, so, as I take the first couple of steps down, I say, "Please call me Logan. No need for formalities."

Your move, Miss Sass.

* * *

Once we arrive at the beach-side restaurant, another open-wall wooden structure, we're the last to join the party. Everyone is here except for the military guys, who must've declined the invite. I can't honestly say that I'm sorry.

There are only two spots left at the table: one next to Tucker, and the other beside Archie.

Without hesitation, Winter bypasses Archie and sits beside Tucker, making me sigh in relief. The last thing I need on this trip is a jungle romance. And I suspect that if Miss Sass and my best friend collided and exploded, things could potentially end worse than in Acapulco. Archie's nickname in college was Lover Boy for a reason, and, unfortunately, he hasn't grown up much since then—not in the romantic department at least.

"What's on the menu?" I ask, taking the chair next to Archie and getting a "does the photographer get hotter every time we see her?" ankle kick under the table. That or he's silently wondering if she's bra-less.

After years of living in symbiosis, as roommates in college first, and afterward on all our adventures around the world, Archie and I have developed amazing non-verbal communication skills.

"I was just suggesting a Thai Experience tasting menu," Dr. Boonjan says to me, pointing out the option on the menu. "It's an authentic roundup of traditional Thai dishes."

We all agree to the suggestion just as a server arrives at our table, notepad in hand. Dr. Boonjan orders for us in Thai. Then, as the server walks away, Dr. Boonjan turns to Winter and asks, "Is this your first time in Thailand, Miss Knowles?"

"Please call me Winter," she says, smiling. "And, no, I've been to Bangkok several times. Also Ayutthaya, Chiang Mai, Chiang Rai, Phuket, Phi Phi Island... but it's my first time in Trat..."

Blah... Blah... Blah... We get it, Miss Sass, you're well-traveled. Join the club.

I tune her out and turn to Archie.

Mistake.

He waggles his eyebrows at me.

I roll my eyes and pick up the wine list. I'm still a little buzzed from the bourbon, and should probably keep my head clear, but enough dry nights await us for me to want to indulge a little while I have the chance.

A citrusy smell hits my nose, and I look up to find Winter spraying lotion all over her bare arms and legs. Across her nape, over her collarbones, down her neckline...

Archie coughs loudly beside me, and this time it's me kicking him.

"What is that?" Tucker asks the photographer.

"Lemongrass spray," Winter says. "A natural insect repellent. You should try it."

Tucker scowls. "That won't be strong enough once we get to camp. You should use the one in the kit."

Winter narrows her eyes, and just when I think she's going to rip into him, she smiles instead and says, "Sure. That's good advice. Thanks."

"No problem."

She's pretending to play ball, but I get the strong impression she doesn't really mean to use the proper spray.

Sassy and stubborn.

What's not to like?

"So," she asks Tucker, "is the lost city location really that wild? What can we expect?"

Each team member had to sign NDAs in order to join the expedition. The documents stressed the need for confidentiality while detailing the perimeter of the mission. But apparently, the classified aspect wasn't emphasized enough. Nor was the importance of the discovery given how casually Miss Sass feels about discussing them. I hate the way she tosses around the words "lost city" as if they were trivial.

Doesn't she get how significant this is?

"I'll brief everyone tomorrow on-site," Tucker says, and then gives her a rundown of the first few days' schedule anyway. "After that," he concludes, "we'll have to play it by ear."

Archie injects himself into the conversation. "That's where my aerial recon skills will come in handy," he says, way too flirtatiously for a work dinner.

"Really?" Winter fires back. "I prefer the nitty-gritty, feet-on-the-ground exploration approach," she shuts him down completely. Not a hint of flirtation in her voice.

I smirk, satisfied, and earn another kick under the table.

"This whole 'radar images and drones' setup is rather unromantic," Winter continues. "What happened to a good old treasure map?"

"Well, we're not treasure hunting," I cut in. "So—"

"And how was your day?" Archie asks Winter, changing the subject while throwing me a chastising, be-nice-to-the-lady side glare.

"Enlightening," she says, a note of sarcasm in her tone. "And unusual."

Three servers arrive, each holding a tray transporting a multitude of dishes. They spread the various bowls evenly across the table and then leave, saluting us with a polite bow.

Archie leans forward to fill his plate as he continues the conversation. "Unusual day? How so?"

"Well, I spent most of the afternoon relaxing by the ocean, which was a nice change," she says, reaching for the mango salad, "but, earlier, I had an emotional long-distance call."

"Boyfriend?" my friend speculates, evidently dismayed.

"No, sister," Winter replies, and Archie perks right back up. "My twin and I hadn't spoken in a while. We're out of sorts... so it was... weird."

"You have a twin sister?" Archie rejoices.

I don't need to look at him to know his mustached lip is twitching in delight.

"Yep."

"She look anything like you?" he asks, aiming for "casual" and failing.

"Yeah, we're identical twins. Why? Oh, please don't tell me you're one of those pervs with a secret fantasy about twins!"

"I'm not a perv!" Archie raises his hands defensively. "Just a man. Every man has a fantasy about tw—"

She doesn't even let him finish before pointing her fork at me. "Logan, do you have a secret fantasy about twins?"

What? How did I get pulled into this?

"No, I don't," I lie, my cheeks heating.

"See?" Winter says sweetly to Archie. "Just you, perv."

Archie promptly rewards me with another kick in the shins.

In an attempt to steer the conversation toward a hopefully less sexually charged subject, I ask, "Why are you and your sister at odds?"

"She slept with our best friend's boyfriend."

I sigh. So sex is inevitably in the picture.

Tucker asks the next question: "Not your boyfriend?"

"No," she confirms.

"So why are you mad at her?" Archie asks.

"You have a brother?" Winter says.

"Yes."

"You're close?"

"Pretty close, yeah."

"Would you get upset if he had an affair with Logan's wife?"

"I'm not married," I jump to say, and get kicked again for the eagerness.

Guess I deserved that.

"His girlfriend, then," Winter says.

"I don't have one of those either," I note, less eagerly this time.

Winter flares her nostrils. "Boyfriend? Husband? Give me something to work with, here, I'm trying to make a point."

"I'm not gay," I say. And for the millionth time today, my face heats up. Everything that comes out of this woman's mouth is thoroughly embarrassing and inappropriate. So much for being a professional, asking me about my sexuality half an hour into our second conversation. This is sexual harassment.

"So," Winter continues, "it's safe to assume you could have a girlfriend, in theory?"

I grit my teeth. "Yes."

"Thank you," she says to me, and then to Archie, "Suppose your brother had an affair with Logan's imaginary girlfriend. Wouldn't you be angry with him?"

"Yes," Archie admits. "But we'd wrestle it out, I'd kick his ass, and once that was taken care of, we'd all get over it. I mean"—he points at me—"the way I see it, if Logan's girlfriend was willing to cheat on him it'd be better if someone ripped the Band-Aid off sooner rather than later."

"Ditto," I say.

Winter shakes her head. "Nah, guys, I'm telling you... to have your significant other and your best friend stab you in the back is not that easy to forgive and forget."

Tucker dips a spring roll into the sweet and sour sauce and asks, "Is your friend still heartbroken?" He takes a crunchy bite.

Winter falters. "No... mmm, actually, Lana, my best friend, is the happiest she's ever been."

I push a suspicious-looking vegetable out of the way on my plate, and say, "How come?"

"She was sort of rescued by the Sexiest Man Alive, and now they're dating."

"Sexiest Man Alive." Archie scoffs. "That's debatable."

"Sorry, Golden Boy." Winter cuts him a sideways look over her Pad Thai. "The man's aesthetic supremacy is certified."

Golden Boy? What is that? Is she flirting?

"How's that possible, Snowflake?" my friend challenges.

Really? Golden Boy, Snowflake? Are they using nicknames now?

Just no.

"Ever read *People* magazine?" Winter asks. "He's on the cover every year about the time when they release the Sexiest Man Alive chart."

"Your friend is dating someone famous?" I ask.

"Yup, Christian Slade," she confirms.

"Oh," Somchai enters the conversation for the first time. "He very good actor. Love his movies."

"Yeah, right?" Winter says. "And he's a pretty decent dude, too."

Archie takes a sip of white wine. "So, come again, why are you still mad at your sister? Is she still dating the other guy?"

"No, she broke up with him because it turned out he was an even bigger ass than just being a cheating cockroach—long story." She waves a hand dismissively. "But that only makes the affair cheaper."

"How?" Tucker asks.

"Because my sister screwed up her life over a douchebag that isn't worth her pinky toe, and now she's a castaway. Everyone knows what happened, thanks to the douche, and she's the one who's ended up having to go around with the figurative Scarlet Letter on her chest. She's all sad and alone... and when Summer suffers, I suffer..."

I have to admit, I don't really care about the soap opera drama and can't help but think women enjoy complicating things for themselves, but that last sentence startles me. "Your twin's name is Summer?" I ask.

"Yes."

"That's—ouch!"

"Sorry, dude," Archie says. "Table's a bit crammed," he adds as a makeshift apology for stomping his don't-mock-their-names boot hard on my foot.

"You were saying?" Winter asks, with a smile so sweet it scares the living daylights out of me.

"Compelling names," I deflect.

She turns her gaze to Archie. "You always have to kick good manners into him?"

Archie throws back his head in a hearty laugh. "No," he admits. "Logan's usually the good boy. I don't know what's got into him today." He arches a mocking brow at me.

"Must be the tropical air," I sulk, polishing the last grains of rice off my plate. My legs are really starting to feel all those kicks. Good thing we're mostly driving tomorrow.

An awkward silence follows.

Tucker breaks it by clearing his throat. "Well, if everyone is finished, I suggest calling it a night. Wake-up call is going to be a bitch tomorrow."

Thank goodness this dinner is over.

Relieved, I throw my napkin on my plate as we all stand up to leave the restaurant.

Winter, heedless of Tucker's recommendation for an early bedtime, steps toward the beach.

"I'll go take a few quick shots by the water and then head to bed like a good girl."

She directs the remark at Tucker, but I know it's really meant for me.

We watch her go, and once her figure is engulfed in darkness, the rest of the group follows the narrow alleyway that leads to the bungalows. At the first fork, Somchai and Dr. Boonjan go right while the Americans proceed left. A few more yards bring us to the next divide, where Archie and Tucker have to follow the right path. Until it's just me walking toward my villa alone.

When I reach it, I stop in the grassy space between my hut and Winter's, undecided if I should wait up until she's made it back safely from the beach. I decide against it. If she wants to be treated like a big girl, then that's exactly what she'll get.

Inside my room, I change, pack the last few things for tomorrow's journey, and jump between the sheets, ready to enjoy my last night in a proper bed.

Between the bourbon, the wine, and the long day, I expect to fall asleep at once... but I don't.

This is stupid. I'm bone-tired, the mattress is comfortable, the temperature perfect... I should've dozed off right away. Also, over the years, I've trained myself to sleep in almost every condition. A necessity with the frequent traveling and less-than-ideal sleeping quarters we usually have on expeditions. In a car, a plane, on the ground with rocks poking my back... I've slept through it all. Once I even slept through the renovation works of the apartment above mine in Berkeley—every morning while I was still jet-lagged for a whole week.

So, really, the moment my head touches the pillow I should be a goner.

But not tonight.

I toss and turn, unable to drift off.

Why? What's bothering me?

Big blue eyes keep popping into my mind, along with the most incredible pair of legs.

Oh, no.

No. No. No.

The photographer has nothing to do with my sleeplessness.

Right.

This trip could make or break my entire career. That's why I'm nervous.

Or the jet lag. I landed in Thailand less than twenty-four hours ago; I'm still on Berkeley time, where it's the middle of the day. That must be it.

No other reason.

Really.

A while later, I hear the rustling of steps outside, followed by the distinct sound of a door sliding open and shut again in quick succession.

So she made it home in one piece.

I let out an exasperated breath and, finally, my lids start to droop...

5

LOGAN

The next morning, I wake up to my alarm with a splitting headache, not nearly as rested as I should be.

Just perfect.

This trip is already proving much more challenging than I anticipated. Let's hope everything will go smoothly today.

In the bathroom, I splash cold water on my face to help my brain catch up with the day's schedule. Then I brush my teeth, shave—who knows when I'll be able to properly do it next—and when I'm done, I drop the last of my toiletries into my backpack, shoulder it, and move outside.

The sky is still midnight blue and the only illumination comes from the path lights lining the walkways. I turn my gaze to the neighboring bungalow.

Everything's dark.

It'd better mean the photographer has already left, and not that her alarm hasn't worked. I'm tempted to go check, but I don't, thinking it'll only prove my point if she shows up late.

Petty, I know, but this woman, for unfathomable reasons, is really getting on my nerves.

When I join the others in the resort's parking lot, Miss Sass is already there and, honestly, looking as jungle ready as the rest of the group.

She's wearing military green cargo pants, black combat boots that rival the ex-Delta Force footwear, and a long-sleeved undyed linen shirt. A different camera from last night hangs from her neck, while her shoulders are weighed down by a gigantic ruck-sack—also military green. Her long hair is pulled back from her forehead into two twin braids that sneak around the side of her head all the way to her nape, where they join again in a thicker, single braid.

"Ogling the photographer, are we?"

Archie's voice makes me jump.

"I wasn't—that's not what..." I scoff. "I'm just glad she didn't show up in a dress."

Archie slaps a hand on my shoulder. "And what do you think of the army look?"

"What do you think?" I ask pointedly.

Archie pulls at his short beard. "Those braids are giving me serious Mother of Dragons vibes, totally hot."

Unfortunately, he's right. I worry Winter Knowles could wear a potato sack and still manage to look totally hot.

"Should I remind you she's off-limits?" I scold.

"Why? Because of your bogus dibs claim?"

"A dibs call is a dibs call."

Archie shakes his head. "Sorry, buddy, but your claim is valid only if you act on it. I'll tell you what." He squeezes my shoulder. "I'll give you a week's head start, but if you don't make a move by next Sunday, then the lady becomes fair game again."

I'm about to protest, but he's already moved on.

"Morning, Snowflake." His deep voice booms across the parking lot. "Ready to rock?"

"Well, hello, if it's not our esteemed drone handler." She beams up at him and raises her camera. "Pose for a departure shot?"

Archie grabs the rear pole of the closest open Jeep and flexes his biceps, stamping a daredevil grin onto his lips.

She brings the viewfinder to her eye and takes a few pictures.

When she lowers the camera again, Archie gestures toward her heavy backpack, saying, "May I?"

She unhooks the straps from her shoulders and lets him load the rucksack on the back of the Jeep.

I roll my eyes and join them before they exchange vows and get married already.

So much for a head start.

"Morning," I greet them.

Winter turns to me, the smile evaporating from her lips. "Good morning," she says, formal and cold.

Then, she eyes me challengingly, as if daring me to find something wrong with her outfit.

But I know better than to take the bait. Every little thing I say to this woman can and will be used against me, so I keep my mouth firmly shut.

"So." She points down at herself. "Is my attire appropriate enough?"

Apparently, she still isn't ready to let it go.

"Top notch," I humor her, unwilling to be pulled into a useless argument.

Her eyes shine with mischief. "Worried I'd show up in a skirt?"

And, despite myself, I discover my lips curling in an amused grin. The lady sure is direct, I'll give her that.

"The thought crossed my mind," I confess. "Glad to see I was wrong."

She gives me a curt nod that I hope means the matter is settled once and for all.

"I told you, not my first rodeo," she says, then turns, yelling, "Shotgun!"

She climbs into the front seat of the Jeep, leaving me with a mental image of her riding a wild horse in cowboy boots—braids and all—permanently ingrained in my brain.

* * *

Winter

After a rocky start yesterday, things are shaping up to run much more smoothly today.

Satan had to basically eat his words about his prejudices toward me, while Archie is really working hard to make me feel part of the team. Although, to be fair, most of his friendliness is probably an attempt to get a sexy thank you from me before the end of the trip. But if he tries something, I'm confident Archibald Hill is the kind of man who can take no for an answer and not be surly about it.

So, all things considered, I'm having a much better time today than I thought possible.

Tucker is driving our Jeep, while Archie and Logan ride in the back. Satan isn't much company at all. He pulled his hat—a wide-brimmed, sable fedora so Indiana Jonesy, I almost asked where he'd left his whip—over his face the moment we took off and has been sleeping with his arms crossed over his chest ever since. Thankfully, Archie and Tucker are better travel companions, and have been very chatty about anecdotes from their previous trips while also telling me more details about the research that preceded this expedition and what they hope to find in the jungle.

I listen carefully as we drive further inland on the dirt road, taking the occasional shot of the thick vegetation surrounding us.

"So," I say, turning back toward Archie and pointing at his seatmate. "Is he always so uptight?"

A struggle between loyalty to his friend and the need to make a smart remark plays on the sweet Viking's face.

Loyalty wins in the end. "This expedition is really important to him."

"Why?"

Before he answers, I catch him and Tucker exchanging a stare in the rearview mirror.

"It's potentially the greatest archeological discovery of the century," Archie says. "Lots of eyes pointed his way. Anyone would be nervous."

"Okay, boys." I shift my gaze back to the road ahead to avoid getting car sick; I can't show any weakness when I'm with Satan, even if he's sleeping. "Cut the bullshit and tell me what you're leaving out?"

Archie is quieter than a tomb. So I train my eyes on Tucker.

He caves under pressure. "It might have something to do with Tara."

"Dude," Archie says. "Not cool."

A woman? Someone who's not cool to talk about... interesting. Could it be the mysterious "she" Archie referred to yesterday? Who is this woman? What happened? What's the story? I need to know.

"Who's Tara?" I ask.

"None of your business," a gruff voice replies from the back of the Jeep.

"Ah, so he lives," I comment sarcastically, spying Logan in the rearview mirror.

He's removed the hat and is now glaring at me—via the car's mirror—very much annoyed. So I let the subject drop. No point in pressuring Satan to share details of his life; it is known all masters of evil are very private about themselves. But at least now I have a name to investigate. I'll have to sweet-talk Tucker into telling me what the big deal about this Tara woman is.

After a few more hours of winding dirt road, we reach the village. It's a bumpy, dusty trip that leaves my back sore.

Tucker parks the Jeep next to a flat, rectangular building that Archie informs me is our rented warehouse. As soon as the car stops, I hop down and stretch my spine and arms like a cat that just woke up from a nap. The others join me in short order.

"Remember," Logan whispers to no one in particular, even if I'm sure he means to remind whatever to me. "Not a word to anyone about our real mission. Always stick to the cover story."

I ignore him and turn to Tucker. "What's for lunch? Any local restaurants come with a recommendation?"

6

LOGAN

We eat a quick meal of brown rice and chicken Pad Thai at the only establishment that serves food in this tiny village of about five hundred souls. The town is built mostly of wooden huts, with dirt roads and only a few brick buildings, one of which is our warehouse. In this kind of landscape, our depot stands out more than I'd like. But it's a small price we have to pay for the safety of having our equipment stored behind secure walls. Honestly, we don't have any reason to suspect anyone of shady dealings, but to stay on the safe side, Dr. Boonjan and I have agreed we have to always assume the worst could happen and stick to our group, talk to as few people as possible, and keep a low profile.

At least, that was the plan.

Unfortunately, by the time lunch is over, news of our arrival has reached the locals. The moment we leave the restaurant, Winter somehow manages to have every kid in town following her around like ducklings. The photographer has a smile for everyone, and I swear she's taking a portrait of every single street urchin. And I'm not suggesting she should be mean to the children, but she shouldn't encourage them. Our escort is quickly turning into a mob. So much for not attracting attention.

Archie bumps shoulders with me. "Try not to look so pissed, it's only kids." He winks at me. "They're not going to take out machine guns and rob us blind."

I scoff. "Yeah, because that never happened."

"That was South America, man," Archie says. "Compared to narco-state, this is Switzerland."

"Let's hope you're right," I say grimly. Before I snap, I busy myself with more practical issues.

I walk toward Somchai, who's standing next to a small herd of mules and horses, and hand him a bowl to-go of Pad Thai. While we were eating, he was arranging our convoy for the last part of the trip to base camp.

I let him gulp down a few forkfuls before I ask, "How's everything coming?"

"All set, Dr. Spencer," he says. "The mules are loaded, and the horses saddled. Nice animals."

"Okay, so we're good to go?"

Somchai quickly finishes his meal. "Ready whenever the crew is ready." His gaze drifts to the wide plaza in front of the warehouse where Winter is still entertaining the small kids, and he gives me a cheeky thumbs up.

I shake my head. So now all I have to do is rein in the photographer.

Lucky me.

I consider sending Tucker or Archie, but knowing them, and starting to get to know her, she'd probably rope them into posing for even more pictures with the locals. But if we want to reach our destination and build our camp before dark, we don't have a minute to spare.

On my way to her, I stop next to Archie. "Call Dr. Boonjan

and the military guys. We're ready to go." Then I sigh and walk into the middle of the plaza, prepared to receive grief. "You should wrap this up," I tell Winter. "The horses are sorted and we need to hit the road."

She gives me a polite look, and I almost expect her to comply with my request at once. But then her eyes shift to the caravan, and quickly back to me, the friendliness gone. "No one's mounted yet."

Always so confrontational. "Yeah, well, we're all mounting now, so"—I make a wide gesture toward the waiting beasts— "whenever you please."

"Okay," she says curtly. "I'm taking another few shots and I'll be right there."

Sure, because the thousands you just took clearly aren't enough.

I bite my tongue and say nothing. I only nod and walk away, careful not to shake my head or give any other sign she's rattled me. Miss Pain-in-my-ass Knowles is making a point of not doing as she's told just for the sake of it. But if I've understood her game, and I have by now, I'm fairly certain she won't be late. She'll wait just enough to annoy me, but not so long as to be the last one on horseback.

Women: what a dreadful species!

True to expectations, our darling photographer asks Somchai to assign her a mount not ten minutes later. Our local fixer chooses a beautiful silver mare for her, whose white mane is only slightly lighter than Winter's braided platinum-blonde hair. I can't help but stare as the woman gracefully hops on the mare and settles in the saddle as if she's done nothing else but horse riding her entire life.

Archie comes up behind me, and I don't need to turn to confirm he's watching the scene with as much awe as myself.

He slaps one arm over my shoulder, and, like the devil he is, whispers in my ear, "And now the Khaleesi fantasy is complete."

* * *

Winter

The horse ride through the jungle is far more pleasant than being jostled around inside a car. Atop my beautiful mare—Duang Jan, which means "moon" in English—I don't feel the fatigue, and the hours pass quickly. I've missed riding, and even when my calf muscles get stiff from lack of practice, I have the best time.

In LA, I always find excuses to not go riding. I'd forgotten how both calming and exhilarating it is to sit on top of a horse. The slow, repetitive rhythm that lets our postures mold one to the other and lets our spirits soar together. When I get back home, I'll find a good riding school and enroll in regular trail rides. I owe it to myself not to forget again how powerfully beautiful it is to mount these creatures.

My granddad from my mother's side taught Summer and me how to ride. Pops owned a farm, and when we were kids we'd spend most of our summers in Indiana, sometimes inviting Lana along. But since Pops passed, we haven't visited. No reason to. My grandmother was too old to run the ranch on her own, so she moved to Pasadena to be closer to my mom. That was years ago, and today's first time I'm back on a horse since then. Definitely too long.

I'm enjoying myself so much that, when we reach the targeted camp area, it feels too soon. My heels are still prickling to give Duang Jan a little push and get wild on a gallop together. Pity the trail never became wide or straight enough to allow us to race the wind. If it did, I wouldn't have been able to behave. I smirk, imagining Logan's face if I had suddenly taken off at a gallop. Satan would've probably thought I'd lost control of my horse and freaked out, maybe burst a coronary. It would've been worth the resulting lecture just to see his expression.

Anyway, the road kept getting narrower, steeper, and more treacherous the farther we advanced, so no chance of a gallop anywhere. Likewise, the jungle became denser with every yard forward, so much so that the area we've stopped in doesn't seem all that hospitable or suitable to build a camp. Yeah, there's the tiniest clearing where we could set up the bigger tents—supplies tent and gathering area—but otherwise, it looks like each individual tent will have to be scattered around where the gaps between the trees allow for enough space.

I jump off my beautiful companion and caress her muzzle.

"You've been a good girl," I tell her. "A very good girl." I tether her reins to a nearby tree trunk.

Behind me, everyone dismounts as well.

Logan and Tucker begin confabulating at once, their voices loud enough to carry over.

"We should get the gathering tent up first," Logan suggests.

"Yeah," Tucker agrees. "And as soon as it's up, I want to brief the group on safety."

"Good idea," Logan says. "Let's be quick about it, then."

And quick they are. I barely have the time to gather and check all my photographic equipment before the tent is up. Tent... the structure is more of a sheltered, open area: four poles holding up a blue tarp ceiling that's also secured to the trees above, creating a sloping roof. Underneath, they've assembled a foldable table and chairs. It's the perfect spot to have a meal or hold a meeting.

"Everyone," Logan calls for attention. "Please gather around, Tucker has a few important announcements."

We all sit around the table—I'm across from Logan with Archie to my right, while Tucker is standing at the head of the table on my left.

"All right, people," Tucker says. "Before we finish setting up camp, I want to stress some basic camping-in-the-jungle safety tips." He sets one foot on the folding chair and leans forward on his bent knee. "First off: undesirable jungle buddies. You can bet the undergrowth around here is teeming with bugs, insects, scorpions, snakes, and spiders. Some venomous, other with bites so painful they'll make you wish to cut a limb off instead of enduring the pain..."

Tucker takes a long pause to ensure everyone's paying attention. "We're equipped with the most common antivenoms and state-of-the-art medical supplies, but we don't know every species that crawls this jungle, and a helicopter would take hours to reach us. So our best bet to stay alive and unhurt is not to get bitten."

That seems a little dramatic. I mean, even when I visited the Borneo rainforest, our guide at the time wasn't half as worried as Tucker. I look around the table to check if everyone else is taking this speech seriously. The soldiers seem mostly unconcerned. Dr. Boonjan, though, has visibly paled. Somchai is sporting his signature cheeky grin. And Logan... is staring "pay attention, woman" daggers at me.

My heart jolts in my chest at being caught absent-minded. So I concentrate back on Tucker and vow not to let my attention wander again. Maybe he's being overcautious, but this is still important stuff to know.

"So, how do we avoid bites?" Tucker continues. "I've provided each of you with a powerful insect repellent; you must apply it all over on a regular basis. Spray your clothes with it, even. And cover up as much as you can, especially after dusk." He fans the air near his face. "Looks like we've gotten lucky, as there aren't too many flies around during the day. But you can bet as soon as the sun goes down, bloodsuckers of all sizes will want to join the buffet, so don't leave any skin unprotected. Use the repellent."

I wrinkle my nose; the spray he provided us stung my nostrils when I smelled it. I'm not letting that chemicals-ridden concoction touch my skin. Don't need a rash, thank you very much. I'm sure my lemongrass spray will—

"Even you, Winter." Tucker's words cut directly into my thoughts. "That natural spray of yours is not nearly powerful enough, and you don't want a case of Dengue fever to prove me right. Understood?"

Morosely, I nod, and stare daggers at Logan as if to dare him to show even the slightest sign of amusement. His face is composed in a too-neutral expression, and he's not looking at me. But I can tell Satan is dearly enjoying me being told off.

"For the same reason," Tucker continues, "I'll spray the perimeters of your tents twice daily. But you must keep the flaps closed at all times—both the internal mosquito netting, and the external rainfly when you sleep. If during the day you want to leave the rainfly open to avoid the tent turning into a sauna, the mosquito netting must still be sealed, always.

"At night, before you go to bed, you must carefully inspect your sleeping bags before getting in. And don't even think of leaving your boots scattered outside your tent. Find a couple of wooden stakes, plant them in the ground, and use them to store your shoes upside down to avoid any unwanted guests crawling in during the night. Each morning, always give your footwear a good shake before you put it on, just in case."

I shiver at the thought of putting my foot in a boot, only for my toes to find something crawly and pinchy inside. Eww.

"If bug bites sting and can transmit diseases," Tucker says, relentlessly carrying on with his terror speech, "a snake bite can turn you into a dead man—or woman—walking right away. So wear your snake gaiters at all times, no matter the hour or where you're going or for however short a journey. Better safe than sorry. Also, if you find an obstacle in your path, don't you ever just walk past it. Go on top first, check what's on the other side, and only then move ahead. Snake fangs can cut through your boots' leather like a knife slicing through butter. Same goes for where you put your hands, be it a branch, stem, or tree trunk—always look before you touch anything. And when you're moving into the jungle, please wear gloves.

"And last but not least." Tucker seems to be finally ready to wrap up the talk of doom. "We have drinking water reserves to last a few days. After that, we'll need to resupply or use the river's water if a journey to the village is not possible. But never drink river water without boiling or sanitizing it with purification tablets first." He eyes everyone around the table with an "understood?" scowl before he goes on. "The river will also be our shower, of sorts; we have biodegradable soap that you can use to clean yourselves. But under no circumstances should any of us leave the camp alone. Always pair up, and ask for an armed escort." Tucker points at our three military men. "Wild beasts could attack at any time, and I don't care if you have a black belt in karate, you're still not taking on a three-hundred-pound tiger with your bare fists and living to tell the tale."

"Hey, pssst," Archie whispers in my ear. "Wanna be my shower partner?"

"Sure."

I agree mostly to enjoy the consequent strained pulsing of Satan's jaw. Logan is so pointedly not looking at us that if he tries any harder, his eyes will roll to the back of his head.

"Ah, yes, one last thing," Tucker concludes. "The local monkeys seem to belong to a crew of petty thieves. Please leave nothing lying around you don't want to be stolen, and always seal the supply tent on your way in and out."

Aha.

Gloating quietly, I turn to Logan once again. Satan's face has turned even stonier, although a faint blush is creeping up his cheeks.

Ha, ha, ha.

I got mine, but you get yours.

* * *

When we're finally dismissed, I ask if I can help with anything, but Logan seems to have had enough of me and tells me a flat no.

Somchai, who, to the contrary, is nice and unprejudiced, comes next to me and asks, "Want to help me with the horses, Miss Knowles? You have good hand with animals."

"Sure," I tell him, happy to have something to do besides hating Satan. "Show me what I have to do."

He brings me to where he has herded the beasts—far enough from the main camp that the smell of their droppings won't reach us—and explains to me what to do. We water and feed the animals, and then Somchai demonstrates how to tether them to each other so they'll be forced to walk one in front of the other, single file. The technique is pretty straightforward, and we make quick work of tying all the beasts together. Tomorrow, he'll escort the horses and mules, except for one, back to the village. It wouldn't make sense for us to keep the animals on the premises and have to feed and water them every day. But we'll keep a mule in case equipment needs to be moved between here and Area X once we reach it.

I retrace my steps to the main camp... and stop dead in my tracks at the scene before my eyes. Logan, Archie, and Tucker have all removed their shirts—so much for staying as covered as possible—and are pulling one tent up after the other. I get why they'd want to risk bug bites and work bare-chested. In the late afternoon, the atmosphere is sweltering and, even shirtless, a thin layer of perspiration covers their backs, making them all shiny.

I try to resist, but quickly give in. Grabbing the ever-present camera dangling from my neck, I stealthily snap a few shots of my sweaty, muscular colleagues. Then I check the results on the small screen on the back of the device, and chuckle to myself. These pictures would look great on an erotica novel, probably one called something like: *Taken in the Jungle by the Three Archeologists*.

Bad me. I shouldn't have these thoughts about my colleagues. But it's impossible to remain impassive in front of such a display of manliness. Even quiet, shy Tucker has a body to be reckoned with. He's less buff than the other two, but still ripped. Where Logan and Archie have Gerard Butler in *300* body types, Tucker is all Spartan Michael Fassbender—he starred in *300* too, only Fassbender wasn't that famous at the time and nobody recognized him.

Still, my gaze can't help but linger on one back in particular. Maybe because I already know what hides beneath the pants, or maybe because the devil must always disguise himself as attractive—to convince people to sell him their souls and stuff. But I can't tear my eyes off Logan. That is, until Archie turns, catches me ogling them, and winks.

Blushing tomato red, I scurry away and claim one of the already-raised tents as my own. Settling myself in and moving all my gear should keep me busy enough, and hopefully keep my mind off half-naked, evil archeologists.

* * *

Unfortunately, with only a foldable cot, a sleeping bag, and my camera equipment to bring in, it doesn't take me long to furnish the tent. Also, Tucker wasn't kidding about the inside turning into a sauna. Even though it's past 5 p.m., and the umbrella of leaves above our heads prevent most of the sun rays from filtering through, the heat is still strong enough to turn these four nylon walls into a sweat trap. So, I fold back the rainproof layer and leave only the mosquito netting to allow as much air to be recycled as possible.

Outside, I string up a clothesline. If we can bathe in the river, I expect the stream can be used to do laundry as well. I choose two trees at the right distance and hang a nylon wire between them. Then, I'm pretty much done setting up, and am already bored. Despite the tiring journey, I'm bursting with all this extra energy. No doubt due to the excitement of being in an unfamiliar place in the middle of a brand-new adventure. I've been on archeological trips before, but never one that involved a discovery of the unknown.

I peek around the camp to check what everyone else is doing. Satan, thankfully, is nowhere to be seen, and neither is his side-kick, Archie. But Tucker—his shirt on once again—is working just across from my tent, setting up the camp's kitchen.

Oh so innocently, I stroll over to him. "What's for dinner?" I ask.

"Tonight, I'm cooking from scratch. Vegetarian Pad Thai," Tucker says, screwing in place the legs of the portable stove he's assembling. "But don't get used to such a Michelin-star treatment."

"Why not?"

"We could buy fresh veggies at the village, but from tomorrow on it'll be mostly 'boil in a bag' food and lots of rice."

"What's 'boil in a bag' food?"

"Freeze-dried, pre-made meals that you boil to rehydrate."

I make a pretend-gag face. "That sounds awful."

"It isn't, trust me. If I hadn't told you, you would've never guessed." Tucker fixes in place a three-sided windscreen to shield the burners. "Plus, with packaged food, we can have as much variety as we want."

"Yeah? Like what?"

Tucker scratches his forehead. "Off the top of my head, we ordered coconut curry beef, pasta primavera, beef stroganoff, chili, chicken lasagna, peanut curry shrimps, stew, spaghetti bolognese, mac and cheese, fettuccini Alfredo, chicken piccata, corn chowder... You name it, we have it." He sighs regretfully. "Except for blueberry pancakes."

"Why don't we get pancakes?"

"Logan thought they'd be excessive."

"What's for breakfast, then?"

"Protein bars, but I stocked all the most delicious flavors— and coffee, of course."

I sulk. Blueberry pancakes sound a thousand times better than all-flavor protein bars. No surprise Satan doesn't love pancakes; he probably doesn't care for marshmallows in his hot cocoa either, and—oh, gosh, is he one of those black coffee drinker types?

I grimace. "Please tell me we have creamer."

Tucker winks at me. "Regular and vanilla."

I let out a relieved breath. "Thank you! And you're right, this is the most variety I've had compared to any other jungle trip."

"Told yah. Plus"—he wiggles his fingers at me—"I add magical finishing touches to every dish. And if not restaurant quality, freeze-dried food is still better than consuming only cold meals, like we did on our first expedition together."

"Okay, Gordon Ramsay, you have the benefit of the doubt." I smile. "So, besides being a 'boil in a bag' chef extraordinaire, what else do you do when you're not on a field trip?"

"I'm an accredited guide at Yosemite, so there's a little of that, then I organize camping trips for kids, and I teach rock climbing on the side."

Ah. The mountain climbing explains the lean, ripped physique.

"How many expeditions have you been on with Logan and Archie?"

"This is our fourth."

"How long have you known them?"

"Three years."

"How did you guys meet?"

"They came to one of my climbing lessons."

"Who's Tara?"

"Logan's ex—No, wait! You tricked me into revealing that info."

I bat my lashes and make an angelic face. "I asked a question, you answered."

Tucker scowls. "You got me comfortable, then fired a million questions at me, and when I was on a roll answering, you asked the one question you knew I wouldn't answer otherwise."

I put my hand to my chest. "Okay, guilty as charged. But you brought her up in the first place, and I had no choice. No one tells me anything; I feel left out."

"Listen, Logan is my friend, besides being my boss, and he wouldn't want me to gossip about Tara—"

"Why not? She dumped him?"

"Yes, but that's not—" I can't hide a little smug smile, and Tucker catches me and gasps. "You did it again! You tricked me into saying more than I should have. What are you, some secret CIA interrogator in disguise?"

"Relax. If you're not going to spill the beans about Tara, I'll go ask Logan directly."

I backtrack a few steps, but Tucker gently grabs my arm. "Please don't, he's just about getting over her."

"Why? Was it an awful breakup?" I ask sweetly.

Tucker flares his nostrils and shakes his head. "You're like a hound that's picked up the scent of the fox." He sighs. "Is there any chance you'll let the topic drop if I don't tell you?"

"Not one," I say.

"Why?"

"For starters, you're making such a big deal out of it, now I definitely need to know."

"But why? What difference does it make to you?"

"I'd like to learn a little more about the people I have to spend weeks alone in the jungle with."

"You're not asking me about Archie's past relationships."

I scoff. "Oh, please, the guy has 'never been in a serious relationship and not interested in one' written all over his face. Am I wrong?"

Tucker seems about to retort something, but then deflates. "No, you're right."

"And anyway," I continue. "I'm asking about Tara only because you implied she's part of the reason Logan is so fastidious about this expedition."

Tucker looks to the sky. "When will I learn to bite my tongue?" He's still holding my arm, and now drags me close conspiratorially. "If I tell you, you promise you won't tell anyone, and that you won't taunt Logan about it?"

I feel like we're in the sixth grade. Should we pinky swear? I'm tempted to ask Tucker, but sense it'd be pushing my luck. So, with a solemn face, I say, "I promise."

"Okay." Tucker lets me go and goes back to assembling the camping stove. "If I have to be drilled, you might as well help me. Hold this." He hands me a bracket component while he screws in place more bolts. "So, Tara. She and Logan were this archeology power couple, going on joint expeditions, working in all the best excavation locations, giving cutting edge seminars, all the shebang. They were the darlings of the community. Everyone thought it was just a matter of time before they got married—"

"How long were they together?"

"They met in college and broke up three years ago."

"You mean, she broke it off. Why?"

"Her career took precedence." Tucker gestures for me to hand him the bracket and gives me the screwdriver to hold in its place. "The year Logan was awarded tenure at Berkeley, she secured enough funding for a project she'd been researching forever... in Egypt."

"Aha. A classic long-distance screw-up scenario?"

"Well, not exactly. Logan wanted to make the relationship work. He has only one teaching semester at UCB, so they agreed she'd go to Egypt and he'd join her for the second part of the year when he was free to do his job from anywhere."

"Then what happened?"

"When his classes were over, Logan went to Egypt as planned, only to return to the States two weeks later, single."

"Oh. Why?"

"As you can imagine, he's not super chatty about it." Tucker pushes a towing handle into the bracket on the grill stand, then pulls on it to make sure it's locked in place. "But the gist is Tara told him she didn't have time for love."

"Ouch," I say, and scrunch my face. "But what's the connection between the breakup and Logan being so obsessed with a lost city in the jungle?"

"Ah." Tucker sighs. "Four months after she broke up with him, Tara unearthed the untouched tomb of Ramses VIII in the Valley of the Kings—I'm talking Tutankhamun level shit. Three years later, and they still haven't finished cataloging everything they found. There are talks about building a whole new dedicated museum in Cairo..."

"Oh, wait, you're right. I saw it on the news a few years ago."

I try hard to remember if a woman was mentioned, but it was too long ago... Even if I'd seen a picture of her, there's no way I could recall Tara's looks. And I can't google her from here. Stupid no-service jungle.

"No kidding." Tucker scoffs. "That stupid tomb was everything everyone could talk about for months... It still is."

I make a skeptical face; once it was clear the site was off-limits to the outside press, I'm pretty sure I spent more time obsessing over the latest celebrity breakup.

Tucker sees my expression and amends, "At least in the scientific community." He picks up the stove's instructions and searches the components scattered on the ground. "Do you see a rectangular tray thingy?"

I pick up a piece and hand it to him. "Like this one?"

"Exactly that." He takes it from me.

"What is it?"

"Drip tray," Tucker says, installing it below the rear of the grill.

Eager to learn more, I return to our conversation. "Okay. So in short, this expedition is a massive, super petty, 'back at you bitch' metaphorical middle finger?"

Tucker can't hide a little smile before he chides me with, "No, it's so much more than an ex-lovers' spat."

"How?"

"Logan is genuinely passionate about his work, and he's spent years researching the legend of the lost city of gold. He has everything at stake on this trip. Screwdriver, please?" I hand the tool over and wait for Tucker to tell me more. He does. "Logan had to put his reputation on the line just to have the aerial survey taken. The pictures alone cost half a mil."

My head explodes. "Half a million dollars?"

"Yep. Now, imagine if this turns into a fiasco. He'd be humiliated. And not just in front of Tara, but every single one of his peers."

"I still believe there's an element of 'I see your pharaoh tomb and raise you a lost city of gold' archeology competition at play here."

"Maybe." Tucker grins. "Logan is only human."

No, he's Satan.

"Done," Tucker announces, screwing the last bolt. "Any other questions?"

"Just one. Why is he so worried? If the satellite images clearly show there's a city beneath the jungle canopy, what could go wrong?"

"Oh, many expeditions have failed before reaching their target location."

"Why?"

"Sudden, unpredictable weather, government upheavals, permits rescinded, too many crew members dying off before the destination could be reached..."

"You're joking?"

Tucker stares me dead in the eyes.

"You're not joking."

His gaze drifts down to my unprotected shins. "Didn't I tell you to wear your snake gaiters at all times?"

I blush. "I thought you meant while we were exploring."

"No, I said at all times, and meant at all times. Now go put them on before you become the first member of this expedition who dies off."

"Yes, sir," I say as my stomach gives a low growl. "How long before dinner?"

"Now that this baby is up"—Tucker pats the stove—"I'll be done in no time."

"You want some help?"

"Nah, you go relax a little... and put those gaiters on."

* * *

Tucker proves he's a wonderful cook with a spectacular Pad Thai. He could give the locals a run for their money.

We eat sitting around the table under the tarp roof, to which they've thankfully added mosquito netting walls. Tucker wasn't kidding; the moment the sun disappeared below the horizon, the camp got swarmed with flying bloodsuckers. They're vicious, especially the tiny ones that are almost invisible and have a stealthy bite you don't feel right away, but that stings like a bitch immediately after. One of those stingers was enough for me to cave and soak myself in the chemical insect repellent.

Once my belly is full, the day's fatigue catches up with me and I'm ready for bed. I say a general goodnight, douse myself in DEET, and brave the short journey to my tent.

The jungle is pitch dark, and the beam of light from my head flashlight—a circular elastic band strapped around my head with a lamp in the middle and another vertical strap crossing from my forehead to the nape of my neck—reveals only a few yards of terrain before me. But it's enough to see where I'm going. Before I get inside the tent, I lower the external layer. The temperatures have dropped, so no risk of getting steamed.

The thin fabric won't provide much protection if an angry tiger decides to claw her way into my tent, but it gives me a false sense of security.

I'm zipping in place the last flap when Archie's voice makes me jump. "Hey, Snowflake."

I turn on him, blinding him with my flashlight. "Don't you ever sneak up on me like that ever again. You'll give me a heart attack."

"Sorry." He winces and moves out of the direct light. Then, with an apologetic grin, he adds, "I brought you stakes."

The sweet Viking is holding two wooden sticks in his hands, about one-inch thick and two-and-a-half-feet long, and he has sharpened one end of each with a knife.

"Oh," I say. "Are we going vampire hunting? Is that what this expedition is really about? There's an ancient covenant of the undead hiding deep in the jungle, and our real mission is to exterminate them?"

Archie blinks, perplexed. "No." He squats down. "These are

for your boots." He picks up a rock and uses it to drive the stakes into the ground. "We wouldn't want you to get in trouble."

I'm not sure if by "get in trouble" Archie means with scorpions crawling into my shoes at night, or if he means with Logan catching me not following Tucker's safety directives. Either way, I'm grateful for my stakes.

"Thanks," I say, and give him a quick hug once he's done.

"No problem, Snowflake," he says, and with a teasing grin, he adds, "And if you get lonely during the night, my tent is two over to your right."

I jokingly push him away. "And you almost made it ten whole minutes without propositioning me."

He puts a hand to his chest, over his heart. "You can't fault a man for trying."

In a mock stern tone, I say, "Goodnight."

"Night."

Archie waves and walks away. I watch him go, sensing we're being observed. The night is too dark to actually see anything further than a few yards, but I can sense a shadow in the darkness watching us and disapproving. Satan is ever vigilant.

Whatever.

I spray the air in front of the mosquito zipper with repellent and then rush in, hoping no insects will dare to follow me inside. I zip myself in and collapse on the cot. Turns out I didn't need those stakes after all. I'm so tired I pass out fully clothed and still wearing my boots.

7

WINTER

Jungle archeological expeditions are boring.

This morning, I followed the vanguard on the first trip inland toward Area X. And, well, if nothing else, now I understand why Logan is so worried about the expedition failing. It has been a punishing ten-hour day of hacking through vines and branches. And we must've covered two, three miles tops. We had to wrestle every inch of the dense vegetation, chopping our way in with the machetes.

I didn't do any actual pruning, since I was documenting the day with photos, but some machete-chopping would have at least broken up the monotony of walking behind the guys at a snail's pace while they waged war on the jungle. Plus, Tucker has forced everyone to wear gloves. And not just any gloves—thick, black, scuba-diving ones that are apparently state-of-the-art to deflect thorns and prevent cuts. Unfortunately, wearing neoprene gauntlets makes pushing the little buttons on my camera super awkward. So, even my favorite activity has turned into a hassle today.

Tonight, the morale around the dinner table isn't the best.

But at least the food is as good as Tucker promised. He cooked freeze-dried mac and cheese, and I can honestly say I wouldn't have been able to tell this wasn't made from scratch if he hadn't warned me beforehand.

"Are you sure there's no easier way in?" Logan asks Archie for the third time since we sat down to eat.

I can't help but roll my eyes for the poor Viking. If Satan is usually insufferable, Satan in a bad mood is a new shade of hell on Earth.

"Dude, I've flown the drone in every direction," Archie patiently repeats. "From above, it all looks the same. Sorry, no shortcuts."

Logan shakes his head, disappointed.

What did he expect? That if he kept on asking the same question over and over again, the answer would suddenly magically change?

Logan switches targets and attacks Tucker next. "We should've brought a chainsaw."

"Man, I've told you already, chainsaws are heavy and need fuel, not to mention permits to be operated in a natural reserve. It would've been a logistical nightmare."

"But at least it wouldn't take us forever to reach Area X."

Archie finishes chewing one last gigantic forkful of mac and cheese and then says, "We planned for a week of jungle hacking. Nothing has changed."

"We projected a week at most," Logan retorts. "At this pace, we're talking a week at best. I can't afford to lose ten days to cover less than fifteen miles."

Dr. Boonjan speaks next. "We should be grateful the jungle is so impenetrable, Dr. Spencer. The terrain's inhospitality has been the only deterrent against the lost city being found and looted in the past."

"Of course, Dr. Boonjan, you're right." Logan's expression doesn't match the kindness of his words.

Dr. Boonjan is lucky he's not one of Satan's friends, or he would've gotten his head bitten off like the others.

Logan glares around the table in search of a new victim. Somchai isn't with us—he left this morning at dawn with the animals, and he'll sleep at the village tonight. He should be back tomorrow. The soldiers are keeping to themselves as usual. And I'm doing my best to be inconspicuous, so as not to give Satan an excuse to yell at me. I didn't do anything wrong, but with him in such a bad mood, I'm sure he'd find something to lash out about.

Out of sacrificial lambs, Logan has no choice but to finish his dinner in silence. Although I imagine he's switched to berating people inside his head instead, judging by his thunderous expression. Thankfully, as soon as he's done eating, he excuses himself and retires to his tent, taking all his toxic energy with him.

The relief must show on my face, because Archie feels compelled to defend his best friend. "Logan is under a lot of stress," he says.

"I didn't say anything," I retort.

Archie grins. "No, but you were thinking it."

"Oh, so now you're a mind reader?"

"Ah, Snowflake, women are such an open book for me." He winks.

"Not gonna happen." I scowl, and then turn to Tucker. "Hey, Wallace?"

"Yeah?"

"Is it true we have a laptop connected to the internet?"

Tucker squirms in his chair, uncomfortable. "Mm-hm, why?"

"Think I could use it to let my folks know I'm okay?"

"The connection is expensive; each crew member gets one hour every week."

"One hour a week, that's all?"

"Yep. If you want to spend yours now, I can bring it over."

"Do I have to use it all at once?"

"Yes, once the countdown starts, it can't be stopped."

"Oh, okay. Now is good, then."

Tucker collects the dirty dishes in a plastic basin—we'll wash them at the river tomorrow—and exits the mosquito netting to return ten minutes later with a rugged laptop.

"Okay," he says. "The connection is timed, a little countdown window will appear by the corner here"—he points to the lower-left corner—"once you log on."

"All right," I say. "I'll write a few emails first, and only connect when I'm ready to send them. How do I go online?"

With a few clicks of the mouse, Tucker opens another window with a red connect button in its center. "Click here and the countdown will start."

"Thank you."

I open a writing app and compose three short emails: for my parents, Summer, and Lana. Then I push the dreaded connection button, triggering the countdown.

59:59.

I log into my email account, check the inbox for urgent messages—there are none, but I have to comb through a flood of unopened spam, wasting so much precious time—and then copy and paste the emails and send them to the respective recipients.

When I'm done, the clock shows I still have time to spare.

32:02.

And since opportunity makes a thief, I could use the spare half an hour to do a little side search. I peek at Archie and Tucker; they're at the other end of the table engrossed in conversation and not paying attention to me. There's no one else around, so I quickly open a Google search page and type:

Tara archeologist Egypt tomb

I'm lucky and get a ton of hits.

About 2,350,000 results (1.00 seconds)

I don't waste time with the articles and click on the image tab right away.

25:48.

Several landscape images of sand dunes and pyramids fill the screen, about half of which feature a beautiful woman with brown hair and blue-green eyes. I scroll for a while, then enlarge two pictures. The first is a book cover. Wearing all khakis, the woman is standing proudly on a dune under the word PHARAOH written in all caps across the page and TARA DOUGLAS printed underneath in a smaller font.

11:23.

The other picture is a headshot. Logan's ex is stunning. She has that girl-next-door adorable look, with cute freckles scattered over her nose and cheeks. But she also appears fierce and smart, and her looks couldn't be any more different from mine.

Why do I care?

I don't!

And I've also run out of time.

2:04.

With a few fast clicks of the mouse, I erase the search history and close all the windows just as the countdown reaches its end.

Phew!

"Managed everything you needed?" Tucker asks.

I shut the laptop and hand it to him. "Yeah, thanks. I'm going to bed now."

Archie immediately stands up. "I'll walk you to your tent."

"It's twenty yards away; I don't need an escort."

"What if you run into a venomous snake?"

I roll my eyes but take Archie up on his offer.

We don't talk on the way over, and when we get to my tent, he only gives me a quick wave, saying, "Night."

I wave back as he walks away.

Standing on the small mat in front of the entrance, I unlace my boots, balancing on one leg then the other, and hook them onto the wooden stakes. Shoes stashed, I repeat the ritual from last night: spray the air with repellent, rush inside, close the rain-proof flaps, and collapse on the cot.

* * *

The next day, I don't bother following the guys in their fight against the thicket. Sorry, but there's only so many pictures one can take of dudes handling a machete. So it's not the alarm that displaces me from my tent, but rather the suffocating heat levels the interior reaches by mid-morning.

After a quick breakfast, I swap jungle trekking with helping Tucker manage the camp. And when Somchai gets back from the village, I help him unload the mule and care for the animal.

In the afternoon, Tucker and I go for a bath, escorted by Montgomery. "Showering", even if I have to do it while wearing a bikini, is the highlight of my day. The water is crisp but not too cold, and a great relief from the oppressive heat of the jungle. Plus, we find a wide, flat rock where we can sunbathe. Without any snakes or wild animals in sight, the soldier leaves us his rifle and he, too, takes a dip in the river.

When the main crew gets back, the general mood isn't much improved. But Logan seems resigned to having to be patient, so dinner goes more smoothly than yesterday, and without Satan berating anyone. Then we go to bed, wake up, and the cycle starts anew in the morning.

Over the next few days, we settle into a routine. Sometimes I follow the guys inland, other times I stay back and help Tucker. The days go by swiftly and, before I know it, an entire week has passed.

That's when disaster strikes.

Our slow but steady progress in the jungle comes to an abrupt stop when we find a wall of solid rock in our path. Short of blowing the embankment off—and we obviously can't since we're in a natural reserve—there's no obvious way forward. With half the day already gone, we retrace our steps back to the base early. Tomorrow, Archie will have to deploy the drone and scout for an alternative route around the obstacle.

But today, everyone takes advantage of the unexpected break. That is, everyone except Logan. I'm walking across the camp to join the others at the river when I spot him bent over a map, studying it intently. He's standing under the tarp, but the sun rays are already low enough to filter underneath horizontally. The light is perfect. It hits Logan's face just right, accentuating the planes and rises of his features. The warm rays crown his disheveled brown hair, giving him a glowing golden halo. The bastard has never looked more handsome.

So unfair.

Cheekbones like that are such a waste on Satan.

Still, the photographer in me can't resist. Of their own volition, my hands reach for the camera slung around my neck and I snap one shot after the other. I capture the small frown of his brows, the barely-there dimple of his chin, the concentrated pout of his lips, the cute freckles scattered across his nose and cheeks... I'm in his thrall. I can't stop.

Suddenly, smoldering green eyes stare directly at me, threatening to smash the camera's lens with the force of their glare.

Click.

This is going to be one fierce shot.

I lower my camera and meet Logan's unfiltered scowl.

"Are you taking my picture?" he demands.

"Yeah," I say, trying to keep cool, but feeling my cheeks already heating.

"Why?"

"It's my job," I snap.

"To take my picture?"

"To document everything. You were standing in a beautiful pose."

He seems surprised and scratches the back of his head. "Yeah, sorry, I don't like to have my picture taken."

I hear the word sorry, but somehow I only get madder. "But of course you hate pictures. Have it your way, but don't come to me when you need a cover for your book."

"What book?"

"The one you're going to write once we find the lost city, of course."

He looks like he wants to be mad, but a smile sneaks onto his face anyway. "You're so sure we're going to find it?"

"Not a doubt in my mind."

"I still don't like having my picture taken."

"Then I'll be sneakier next time."

As I turn to walk away, he says, "I never said I was writing a book."

"No, but you will," I say. Then, I add in a mutter, "Tara did."

Logan stalks after me. "What did you just say?"

I stop and turn to face him again. "Nothing."

He's wearing a strangely satisfied expression as he regards me, all hands-on-the-hips smug. "I should tell Tucker you only need half an hour on the internet this week, considering you had time to waste researching my ex."

My jaw drops with outrage. And I hate him for connecting the dots so quickly, busting me for using the precious satellite connection to research Tara. "You're the most insufferable man I've ever met."

Satan flashes me a cocky grin I haven't seen before, and says, "I'd say I'm intriguing, considering you went to all that trouble to find out about my ex." He gives me a mock military salute, adding, "Have a nice bath," and goes back to studying his map.

Fuming, I march toward the river where Tucker and Archie and our armed escort are waiting for me. When I get there, Tucker is already in the water, while Archie is showing off his sculpted physique on a flat rock while he undresses. The man can sure work a pair of board shorts.

I join him on the rock and start shedding all my clothes except for the bikini I'm wearing underneath in curt, angry motions. Mentally, I'm reliving my exchange with Logan.

What a pompous prick!

I can't believe the nerve of that man.

I'd say I'm intriguing...

Intriguing, my ass.

Unbelievably annoying, maybe. Impossible, full of himself, overconfident... those are adjectives I would use. Not intriguing.

"Hey, Snowflake," Archie cuts into my mental rant. "From the way you're huffing and puffing, I can only guess you've just come from an encounter with Logan."

"Ah! I don't understand how you can be friends with him. He's evil."

Archie smiles, unconcerned. "I've already told him, and now I'm going to tell you, too. You guys should get over yourselves and just do it."

"Do what?"

"Seal the deal, get some, bone each other… Call it as you may, but please get a move on."

I stare at him, shocked. "Are you out of your mind? Every time I talk to him, I can't go five minutes before I want to kill him."

Archie winks at me. "It's the sexual tension, honey. Trust me, just get it out of your system and you'll feel better."

I glare at him. "How come you're not volunteering to blow off steam together anymore?" I ask.

I preferred when he was hitting on me every five minutes rather than pushing his annoying best friend on me.

"It's clear I'm not your cup of tea, Snowflake," Archie says, taking a step back toward the edge of the flat boulder. "And hate sex can be amazing."

I twirl a finger next to my temple. "You está loco."

"I've got 100 dollars here that say you'll bang him before we get out of this jungle." Archie turns and runs the remaining length of the rock, screaming as he races and then jumps.

Splash!

I run and jump after him. "And I have 200 dollars that say I wooooon't!"

8

WINTER

Mid-morning, the next day, a commotion in the camp makes me miss the perfect shot of a mama monkey jumping from one tree branch to another with her baby macaque fastened underneath her belly.

Annoyed, I walk the few paces back to the tent enclosure to check what's going on.

At once I spot Tucker and Somchai dragging a moaning Archie between them. He seems to have trouble walking on his own. Also, with each step, a subdued cry escapes his lips.

I run to them. "What happened?"

Tucker looks at me. "A bird flew into the drone and knocked it out of the air. It got stuck in a tree, and Archie climbed up to retrieve it."

With a visible effort, Archie raises his head, his face ashen. "And then I fell ass-first into a thorn bush."

"A thorn bush?" I ask, perplexed.

"Jungle can be tricky," Somchai explains. "Evil plants. But we saved plane." He shows me the little flying robot in his other hand.

Logan joins us, carrying one of the folding cots from inside a tent that he places under the tarp. "Lay him here."

They gently lower Archie onto his stomach, causing further protests, and at once it's clear his injuries are serious. The whole rear side of his trousers is stained with blood, the fabric is ripped in multiple places, and are those thorns still sticking out of his flesh?

"You didn't remove the thorns before moving him?" I accuse.

"With what?" Tucker shrugs. "I was afraid I'd do more damage with my unclean hands, cause an infection or something."

"Well, you can do it now. I'll go grab the first-aid kit."

Kit is an understatement; the case I bring back is a portable mini hospital loaded with everything from basic gauzes and disinfectant up to an out-and-out surgical starter set.

I hold the heavy case in my hands and offer it to the men. "So, who's going to do it?"

"I will," Tucker says, taking the case from me. "But I need assistance."

"I can help," Logan offers.

Tucker eyes him dubiously. Logan's face has turned positively greenish.

"Does the sight of blood make you queasy?" Tucker asks.

"A little," Logan admits.

"Then you better get outta here. I don't need my assistant to pass out on top of everything else."

Tucker turns to me, raising his eyebrows questioningly.

I could back off and ask one of the military guys to help fix Archie's butt. I'm sure they wouldn't have problems stomaching the work, but I also sense they wouldn't be the gentlest, so I offer to help instead. "I can do it," I say.

Logan nods at me in a silent thank you, throws one last stare at his suffering best friend, and regretfully but necessarily walks away looking nauseous.

Somchai lifts the heavy plane still in his hands as a way of apology, saying, "I'll put this in supply tent. And I need feed the mule."

A small bow and he's gone, too.

Tucker opens the case and squirts a generous amount of sanitizing gel onto his hands and then passes the small plastic bottle to me. "Let's make sure our hands are clean first."

I take the bottle from him and mimic his actions massaging the gel onto my palms, fingers, and the back of my hands.

Once I'm finished, Tucker hands me a pair of blue surgical gloves. "Here, wear these."

Gloves on, we kneel next to the camp cot and stare at Archie's backside, undecided on how to proceed.

Tucker sighs. "Before I do anything, I need a clear visual. We have to remove your pants and underwear to do a decent job, buddy," he informs the patient. "Might be best to cut them off you."

"I'll take care of that," I say.

Archie groans. "I swear, Snowflake, in all the scenarios I'd imagined you ripping my clothes off, a medkit wasn't involved."

"I bet not." I grab a pair of surgical scissors out of the case, douse them with disinfectant, and, holding the first tendril of fabric from Archie's pants between my fingers, I say, "Now, try to relax."

* * *

Logan

Winter and Tucker spend close to two hours cleaning and bandaging Archie up. When, finally, there's no more blood in sight and my friend's backside is modestly covered with a white sheet, I go and check on him.

Tucker has already left to clean and sanitize the instruments they used, so I find only Archie and Winter under the tarp.

"How are you, buddy?" I ask him.

"I could use a drink," he mumbles.

Well, if he's asking for alcohol, then everything is fine.

"Let's see what the doctor has to say," I tell him. "So." I turn to Winter. "How's the patient doing? Can he have a drink?"

"Yes." She groans, getting up from her kneeling position next to the camp bed and stretching her legs. "If it's water."

Archie moans in protest.

"We gave him an antibiotic to prevent infection and parac-etamol for the pain. Mixing alcohol and medications is never wise. You were pretty messed up, Golden Boy. Must've fallen on a thousand thorns."

"Felt more like a million," Archie complains.

Winter raises her arms above her head and stretches some more while she keeps giving me the patient's prognosis. "Some were still inside, stuck in deep, but I think we got them all out."

"So he's going to be fine?"

"Don't talk about me as if I'm not here," Archie objects.

Winter ignores the remark. "He should be. But some wounds were deep; we had to stitch a few."

"We? You know how to give stitches?"

She turns to me with her usual contempt. "Yes, I did a few when Tucker's hands started to cramp. And don't look so surprised. I visit the most remote places on Earth often enough to know basic medical training could make the difference between life and death."

Why does this woman have to take everything I say as a personal offense?

"I was merely trying to say I was impressed with your medical skills, Miss Knowles. No need to take everything so personally."

"Maybe I wouldn't if everything you've ever said to me hadn't been—"

"Kids," Archie interrupts us with a coarse voice. "I'd like to rest; can you go argue someplace else?"

She crouches near the front of the bed and caresses Archie's hair back in such a tender gesture, my chest clenches.

It's not jealousy, but a more complex emotion. A tangle I can't describe. Seeing her being so attentive with my best friend makes me cherish and resent her at the same time.

"Yeah, you'd better sleep now, Golden Boy," she says, still caressing his hair. "And don't try anything stupid when you wake up."

"You mean something dumber than climbing above a thorn bush?"

"Yup, like trying to get up or walk on your own. You're on bed rest for a few days, all right?"

"Yes, Mom," he replies.

And a breath I hadn't known I'd been holding leaves my lungs. Nothing in this interaction reeks of sensuality. It's affectionate, but not sexual.

Winter stands up again, and I jerk my chin toward the other side of the camp.

We head that way and, in the shade of my tent, I ask, "You really think he'll be okay?"

"If he takes it easy, yeah, he should be."

"Wouldn't it be more prudent to send him home?"

"Unless you can fly a helicopter out here to pick him up, I

don't see how. Walking is out of the question, as is sitting on the back of a mule. And even if he somehow were to reach the village without tearing all his wounds open, the Jeeps' backseats don't have enough room for him to lie down comfortably."

"No, you're right. I'm just worried. Archie isn't the best at not being able to do things on his own."

"You'll have to make him accept our help. The stitches should be solid, but it won't take much for them to burst if he tries something stupid."

"Okay, I'll make sure someone always stands discreetly by his side, at least for the next few days."

"Are you stopping the search in the meantime?"

"No, I can't afford to stall, not even for a day. Archie took enough aerial surveys to find a way around the rock wall. Tomorrow morning, I'm setting out with Somchai and Dr. Boonjan at first light. We're close now. With a bit of luck, we could reach Area X by nightfall. Tucker will stay behind and take care of Archie."

"Good." Winter nods. "'Cause I'm coming with you." She says it with such finality, I know there's no point in arguing. "I want to be there when you find the city."

9

WINTER

The trek the next day is hard. With the first stretch of jungle inland already cleared of vines and undergrowth, Logan is setting a punishing pace. I swear he's doing it to provoke me. To force me to ask for a break or for him to slow down, most likely to tell me that if I can't keep up, I'm welcome to go back to the camp and wait there.

Fat chance!

If today's the day we finally reach the gold city, I won't be left behind. I'll be damned before I miss capturing the moment. Finding a legendary lost civilization in the jungle won't be career-making only for Logan. We'll be the first humans to set foot in the forgotten place in over a millennium. My pictures will be the only photos of it. The news of the discovery is bound to blast through every information network in the world: newspapers, magazines, newscasts, websites... My shots will appear everywhere. I'm going to be famous.

Right! You're not shaking me off, Satan.

I can already picture *National Geographic* asking me to be a regular correspondent. I'll set up a pop-up gallery in LA to display the best shots, and the exposition will become such a raging success, it'll move to New York next, then London, Paris, Milan...

As eager as I am to reach that level of international recognition, first comes the hard part. The camera equipment is heavy on my shoulders and it's weighing me down. I shrug, readjusting my backpack to cut my aching trapeziuses a break, and trudge forward. Thank goodness Somchai and his mule are carrying the rest of the supplies: sleeping tents, water reserves, and Logan's mysterious archeological tools.

As the morning progresses, things get worse. Leaving at dawn, if not fun, at least spared us the worst of the heat. But now, three hours into our little stroll through the jungle, the temperature has become insane. Even if we're not standing in direct sunlight, the humidity trapped beneath the canopy makes it hard to breathe. It feels like walking through solid air. The moisture clings to my clothes, mixing with sweat so that everything I'm wearing—down to the socks in my boots—is damp. Even though I've tied my hair back in twin French braids, small tendrils have escaped and stick to my forehead regardless of how many times I push them back. Not to mention I have to hike through this hell of a place wearing gloves and Kevlar leg warmers—the snake gaiters.

I get the need for the gaiters, I really do, even if we haven't spotted a single venomous snake since we've arrived, but I can't stand the gloves anymore. I peel them off my hands and let my skin breathe some well-deserved air.

Gosh, I really hope today is it. That there's a shiny golden city waiting for us at the end of this hike. I wouldn't want to start over tomorrow. Heck, I probably wouldn't be able to even if I wanted; my legs would not carry me. Tramping through the deepest, darkest parts of the Thai jungle is not my idea of a good time.

I'm so over the forced march that when, twenty minutes later, Somchai suddenly stops at the head of the column, I almost sag to my knees with relief. A wall of tangled vines and branches is blocking the road ahead. It appears we've reached the end of the cleared path. If we have to start hacking our way through, I can finally rest a little and let the boys play with their machetes.

Smith and Carter, our militia escort, take the first shift and start hacking at the tangle of vegetation, slicing through the thicket in short order.

There's only the five of us today. Dr. Boonjan wasn't feeling well this morning, a stomach bug or something, and he remained at the base. Tucker had to stay back to care for Archie. And Montgomery is with them to guard the camp.

Groaning, I strip off my backpack and lower it to the ground. I sit at the foot of an old, gnarled tree, its tall, thick trunk soaring into the air until it joins the blanket of leaves far overhead, a merciful screen that lets only a few patches of sunlight filter down.

Somchai, my guardian angel, offers me a water canteen before he goes back to attending the mule. The animal is getting restless after the abrupt break.

Head tilted up, I gulp down the liquid in long, greedy sips.

"Slow down," a familiar voice says. "We don't know how long the water has to last."

Arms crossed over his chest, Logan is observing me while leaning against a nearby tree.

I glare at him, and he rewards me with a mockingly sweet smile. "Are you enjoying the jungle stroll?" he asks, eyes twinkling.

Before replying, I study him. He can't be faring much better than I am. The hair on his forehead and at the back of his neck is sticky with sweat, and his shirt has more damp patches than dry spots. And, damn me, the son of a bitch has never been more good-looking.

Anyway, I'm too tired to argue with him right now. So I give him a tension-defusing answer.

"I'll be honest," I say. "Crap as it was, I'm sorely missing the resort's air conditioning."

Logan gapes, taken aback by my sincere, unchallenging reply. "Yeah." He nods. "Every time I breathe I feel like I'm standing in a steam room."

We stare at each other, both surprised at how civil our exchange has turned out to be. When the silence becomes awkward, Somchai mercifully breaks it by coming back to fetch his canteen.

"More water, Miss Knowles?"

And even though I could drink my weight in water right now, I refuse the offer. "No, we'd better save our reserves, we don't know how long they have to last."

I wink at Logan.

He shakes his head as Somchai bows and scurries away.

Cracking a smile—damn, that's a good smile—Logan pushes off the tree and offers me a hand—also glove-free—to get up. "Time to go. Smith is hacking through the vines like a human chainsaw. We don't want to lose him."

I clasp hands with him and allow him to pull me up. When we come face to face, I can sustain his curious gaze only for a few seconds before I let go of his hand and bend again, breaking eye contact to retrieve my backpack. I drag it over my shoulders once more with a grunt.

"Heavy?" Logan asks.

"Yeah, the camera equipment isn't exactly feathers."

Logan beckons. "Give it here."

"What? No! You can't possibly carry two."

"I'm not going to; I'll see if Somchai can fit it on the mule's back."

Astonished by the kind gesture, I unsling the backpack, take out my main camera, and hand the rest to Logan. "Thanks."

He gives me a curt nod and walks away with my equipment. Who knew? Even Satan has a heart.

Break over, we resume walking single file down the narrow path cleared by Smith. But our pace now is remarkably slower, and with my back unencumbered, I can finally enjoy the scenery in all its hostility.

The jungle has gotten thicker, more tangled. Torn branches and vines claw at us from either side of the trail, and I have just enough space to raise the camera and snap a few shots.

Somchai whispering comforting words to the mule while pulling the beast forward.

Smith swinging the machete, the blade catching a sunray.

Logan, sleeves rolled up, wiping the sweat from his forehead with his machete-free arm.

Logan, pushing a cane out of the way.

Logan, staring daggers at me because I'm taking his picture again.

These will look fantastic on an expedition reportage.

For three more hours, we venture deeper into the jungle, slipping into territory unknown to mankind for a thousand years. Until the ever-thickening rainforest finally seems to thin away, making our advance easier.

Machetes back in their sheaths, we trudge on for another hour before Logan halts, raising a hand to signal for us to do the same.

He stands so still that, for a moment, I wonder what's the matter. In front of him, a peaked mountain covered in even more vegetation blocks the way. Is he pissed about yet another obstacle to bypass?

But Logan seems transfixed, turned to stone where he's standing. With a few strides, I'm next to him, ready to ask what the holdup is, when I notice the glistening in his eyes.

I follow his gaze toward the hill, not sure what has moved a grown-ass man to tears. Then a rare gust of wind rustles the branches overhead. The light shifts, and, underneath its blanket of vines, the mound seems to sparkle as if it was made of solid— holy crap!

"Is that gold?" I ask.

Not averting his eyes from the incline, Logan nods, sinking to his knees.

He makes for a beautiful image, the gorgeous, teary-eyed archeologist prostrated before his discovery. The photographer in me wants to immortalize the moment, but the woman decides it's too private for the world to witness. This is Logan's moment. And his alone.

* * *

Logan

After years of research spent enduring the skepticism of every single one of my colleagues... The gossip, the snickering comments about me having gone mad after Tara left... Tara's own reservations delivered by email; she couldn't even bother to call... I'm looking at the legend: the lost city of gold.

The city is real.

Well, sorry to all the big heads of the archeology community; you'll all have to eat your words.

Brushing tears of joy—of vindication—away from my eyes, I stand up and approach the building in front of us. With my bare hands, I tear at the vines covering the exterior. Some come off easily, while other thicker, more gnarled ones require me to pull with all my strength, but I can't risk using the machete and damaging the treasure underneath. So I fight with the vegetation until I've cleared a surface of three square feet, revealing the head of a scaly, horned creature, its features contorted in a terrifying snarl.

A guardian dragon.

"Hello, my friend," I say to the beast, gently patting its pointed teeth.

At once it's clear the statue isn't made of solid gold, but rather stone painted gold or covered with gold foil. Still, the effect such a monumental construction will have once the vegetation blanket is cleared off will be unprecedented. A sight like no other.

A click next to me makes me turn, and I find Winter dutifully snapping pictures of the dragon head, and of me, too.

I scowl.

But the damn woman grins at me and immortalizes my frown.

What part of "I don't like to have my picture taken" wasn't clear, I wonder.

Anyway, Winter's interruption reminds me the others are here. I've been so absorbed by the temple in front of me, I'd forgotten. But now I turn to them. "Somchai," I call.

His mule tethered to a tree, our local guide is next to me in a few quick strides. "Yes, Dr. Spencer."

"We need to set up camp for the night. Please see to that."

Somchai bows his assent.

"Then tomorrow, I need you to go back to the main camp and show Dr. Boonjan the way. He should be recovered by now and he'll want to see this. And Tucker, too, if Archie can manage on his own. We need to establish a permanent secondary camp here. You think you can make a return trip in one day?"

"Two days," Somchai says. "One to go, one to come back."

Not the answer I'd like, but if Somchai says two days, it can't be done any quicker.

"All right," I say. "When you have the camp arranged for the night, please come help me."

Somchai bows and scurries away.

I turn back to the building and flex my hands, ready for some more hard work. Clearing centuries of undergrowth is going to be a bitch. The skin on my palms feels tender just thinking about it.

"Somchai?" I call.

"Yes, Dr. Spencer?"

"Do we have working gloves in the equipment?"

I need real work gloves; I can't do this wearing Tucker's stupid scuba-diving ones.

"Let me check," Somchai says.

He rummages inside the mule's sacks and then comes back, handing me two pairs of what are basically gardening gloves. Perfect.

I don one pair, and flap the other in my hands, eyeing Winter.

She's been fluttering around this entire time taking pictures.

Now she must sense my gaze on her, because she promptly turns, asking, "What?"

I flap the gloves one more time and offer them to her. "Care to help?"

Her eyes widen, while her mouth pouts into a cute little "O" shape.

Did I say cute? I meant annoying.

"You expect us to clear the whole building by hand?"

Yeah, definitely meant annoying.

"No, a dedicated team will have to do the work later," I explain patiently. We're in a truce, and I'm not about to jeopardize that. "But I want to remove as many vines as possible at the base and see if we can find an entrance."

Now she claps excitedly and takes the gloves from me. "This is so like an *Indiana Jones* movie."

I roll my eyes but can't suppress a little smirk at her enthusiasm.

She carefully sets her camera on a nearby rock and, side by side, we attack the vegetation. It's hard work, and we're already exhausted from the day's trek. So, when our efforts finally reveal an opening, we don't have the strength to explore further. Eager as I am, it wouldn't be safe. We pause for the night, eat a cold dinner, and I don't even have to bully anyone to go to bed early.

* * *

The next morning, the camp stirs awake at the crack of dawn. Everyone is eager to clear the building entrance and discover what lies underneath. After a quick breakfast of black coffee and protein bars, Somchai and Carter leave with the mule to go back to the base and bring the others and more supplies, leaving me, Winter, and Smith behind.

While Smith is busy "securing the perimeter"—his ready-made excuse to avoid any hard work—I clear the entryway of the remaining vines and weeds while Winter documents my efforts.

Without the risk of hitting stone, I hack at the residual vegetation with the machete at double speed.

Once the job's done, we all stare at the dark opening. It's framed by a solid stone arch, and not a sliver of light comes from within.

"All right." I break the silence. "Time to go in."

I pick up two headlamps from the supplies Somchai left behind and hand one to Winter. She adds it to her basic gear: a survival-essentials backpack equipped with food, water, a first-aid kit, and whatever else Tucker put inside; and the camera never missing from around her neck. I don my own survival backpack, secure the headlamp across my forehead, and turn back toward the soldier. "Hey, Smith, you coming?"

"I'd better." Hands never leaving the precious rifle strung across his chest, he spits on the ground. "In case you find something funny in there."

"Great," I say, even if, to be honest, Smith is so creepy I'd feel safer without him. I pick up the last backpack and hand it to him. "Take one of these. Sorry, but we don't have any more flashlights."

Smith shrugs, his beady black eyes darker than the emptiness beyond the passage. "Sure."

"If we keep close, the light should be enough for everyone to proceed safely."

The hired gun nods.

Standing at the edge of the portal, Winter and I turn our headlamps on and, exchanging a nod, we plunge into the passage.

10

WINTER

The headlamps cut two slivers of light into the unforgiving pitch-darkness ahead. We proceed cautiously along a narrow corridor wide enough to admit two people walking abreast. Logan is by my side, and the echo of Smith's steps behind us tells me the creepiest guard ever is following suit.

Besides being black as night, the confined space is also eerily quiet, except for the sound of our feet dragging on the floor. When the flutter of a sudden rush of wings flies past us, it scares me witless.

"Aaargh!" My scream bounces off the stone walls. "What was that? Something hit me in the face."

"Just bats," Logan says.

"Just bats?" I repeat. "'Cause that's so comforting."

"It's an abandoned, dark cave." Satan scoffs. "What did you expect?"

"Oh, I don't know. Should I look forward to pits filled with snakes, too?"

"Please, this is not a literal *Indiana Jones* movie." Logan pivots, blinding me with his headlamp. "I doubt the place is booby-trapped."

I stop walking and raise a hand to shield my eyes. "Hey, point that thing some other way," I say, and when he does I add, "You doubt we'll find booby traps, or are you sure we won't?"

Logan stops a step ahead and turns back to me, orienting his light toward the wall. "Again, this is not a movie, so it's improbable—"

"Ah, but not impossible!"

"Listen." Even if I can't see under the light's glare, I know he's rolling his eyes. "If the statues outside are any indication, this should be a place of worship. Like a church. How many churches do you know with booby traps?"

"Still, I'd rather not have my head cut off by giant rotating blades dropping off the ceiling."

Logan shakes his head. "You really watch too much TV. Worst we're going to find is a maze."

"And you're not worried we'll get lost?"

"No. Because I'm marking the way in." He directs the flash-light beam toward the wall to his right, illuminating a small arrow he must have drawn in white chalk. "But if you're too afraid to come along," Logan continues, "you can pass your head-lamp to Smith and head out. No one's forcing you to be here."

I purse my lips. "I'm not staying behind."

"Okay, then."

Without further comment, Logan moves forward.

I follow him, but now I trail a few steps back. Just in case...

In the darkness, it's hard to tell distances. But when, so far as I can judge, we've gone some fifty paces, the obscurity gives way to a faint light. Another minute, and we enter the most wonderful place I've ever seen.

An atrium vast and tall like a hall in a cathedral, only windowless. The dim light comes from above, presumably through shafts connected with the outer air and driven into the roof, which arches away a hundred feet above our heads. We're standing in an enormous single aisle, loftier and wider than in any church I've visited. Running in twin rows down the length of the nave are gigantic pillars that shine even in the semi-darkness. Contrary to the exterior of the temple, they appear to be made of solid gold. No matter how impossibly heavy they must be, they soar up to the distant ceiling with a delicate beauty. The tops of the pillars are decorated with sculpted capitals, and the main posts are carved with flowers and leaves that climb up and around to the head of each column.

I try snapping a few pictures of the place, but the images that appear on my camera screen are only a poor imitation of the magnificent chamber. No matter how many times I adjust the exposure and focus, nothing comes even close to the real thing.

As we make our way further into the temple, three more pillars take form at the end of the aisle, placed horizontally across its width. Only, as we draw closer and the shapes get better into focus, they transform from simple cylindrical columns to three colossal forms standing upon huge pedestals of dark rock. With human bodies and monstrous faces, each gold statue measures about thirty feet from the crown of its head to the pedestal, and they're separated by a distance of about forty paces.

Logan points his flashlight at the figure furthest to the left, and whispers, "Garuda."

The statue has the torso and arms of a man, and the wings, head, beak, and talons of a bird of prey.

"Um, who's this charming fella?" I ask.

"Garuda," Logan repeats. "The legendary bird-like creature, a guardian with the power of traveling anywhere."

"So he's one of the good guys?"

"They all are." Logan shifts his gaze, along with the beam of his light, to the statue in the center. "This is Yasha. He or she..." Logan lowers his gaze to the sculpture's chest area. "She, then... is another guardian deity, mostly benevolent."

"Mostly?" I ask. "What does she do when she gets angry?"

Logan gives me a cheeky grin. "She devours nosy travelers."

Smith knocks on the statue's feet. "Well, at least the man-eating bitch is made of solid gold. Hollow by the sound of it, but it must still weigh a few tons. Pity they didn't make smaller versions we could bring home as souvenirs." The soldier lets out a low chuckle.

Logan scowls at him. "Everything we find here belongs in a museum."

"Yeah, sure, Professor." Smith shrugs. "Just saying the bitch is valuable."

The boys are still glaring at each other, so, to defuse the tension, I ask, "And what about the last one?" I stare up at the third statue, illuminating its devil face. "He doesn't look friendly to me."

"That'd be Mock," Logan says. "He is a monkey god of justice. Together, they're a powerful trinity of guardians."

"And what are they supposed to guard?" I ask.

"Very good question, Miss Knowles." Logan turns to me, and then back to the statues. "Why don't we go find out?"

Our lights cut through the darkness behind the colossi, but they meet no wall. The main aisle seems to open onto a smaller cave, just as a lesser chapel opens out of a great cathedral.

"Shall we?" Logan asks.

I nod and follow him to the end of the vast and silent cavern, where we find another doorway—not arched like the one at the entrance to the temple, but square at the top.

"Rather ghastly," I say, peering into the dark passageway.

"Come on, don't tell me you're getting cold feet now?" Logan teases, and politely makes room for me to take the front. "Ladies first?"

"Hell no."

"All right." Logan chuckles and once again leads the way into the darkness.

This passage is smaller, and we have to proceed single file. Logan in the vanguard, me in the middle, and Smith taking the rearguard. The only sound is that of our feet scraping the dusty floor, and I can't help being overcome by some unaccountable bad presentiment. Like something evil is awaiting us on the other side of the tunnel.

After about twenty paces, I'm beginning to feel claustrophobic when, thank goodness, we reach a wider space. We're in a gloomy, rectangular room forty feet long by thirty across, and about thirty-five feet in height. This area doesn't have natural lighting like the main hall, but at least there's enough room to breathe, giving my mounting cabin fever a rest.

The last thing I want to do is admit to Satan that I'm scared. So I concentrate on our surroundings. It doesn't take long for my eyes to grow accustomed to the dimmer light and make out the contents of the new chamber.

The center of the room is taken over by a massive stone table with a gold figure lying across its length. A reclining Buddha.

The statue is on his right side, head resting on a cushion with an arm folded underneath.

Even if the surrounding atmosphere has a slightly grim feel to it, the figure looks serene.

Still on edge, I babble the first thing that comes into my head. "Great place to take a nap, I guess."

"This is a representation of Buddha's last illness," Logan says. "He is awaiting death to enter nirvana."

"Cheery." I chuckle nervously. The statue reminds me of the reclining Buddha I saw in the Wat Pho temple in Bangkok.

"This is a work of art," Logan says, circling around the table to inspect every inch of the sculpture. "Centuries-old, as ancient and beautiful as his guardians outside... Same artist, I reckon."

"So you think the jolly demons outside are there to protect him?"

Smith regales us with one of his rare conversational pearls. "Nothing else of value in here, Doctor?"

"Nothing else?" Logan gapes, shocked. "This is the discovery of the century! The beauty, the craftsmanship it must have required to sculpt something so magnificent—"

"All right, Professor," Smith interrupts, "no need to get all worked up. I was just wondering if we should search for a hidden treasure chamber or something."

For the first time, I notice the room is a dead end: stone walls all around and nowhere else to go. Logan seems to realize it at the same time I do, because he spins on his feet to examine each of the walls in turn. I follow his lead and brush my fingertips on the stone of the left wall. The entire surface is carved with decorations similar to those on the pillars outside. But while the two side walls are flat, the one at the back has a wide, square recess in its middle. Just tall enough to fit a man.

That's where Logan stops his focus and beam of light.

"Well, well," Smith says. "What do we have here... If it doesn't look like the entrance of a secret passage."

In synchrony, we all approach the blocked opening.

Logan traces its corners with his fingers. "Definitely a separate slab," he says. "There must be a hidden mechanism some-where to activate it."

I cross my arms and raise a skeptical eyebrow. "Really? Kind of a heavy door to move without a power source."

"Indeed," Logan agrees. "A stone like this must weigh at least twenty or thirty tons. But, contrary to booby traps, secret passages were pretty common in ancient buildings. They were triggered by a wide number of counter-weight mechanisms that relied on simple balance principles to move even the greatest masses." Still searching the stone with his hands, Logan adds, "All we have to do is find the switch."

"If you say so," I reply, even more skeptical.

Arms crossed over my chest, I lean against the side of the cave to watch Logan in his fool's errand, but as my shoulder comes into contact with the wall, the rock doesn't stay put.

A carved disk about ten inches in diameter sinks inward, then stops with a loud click.

And then the stone door begins to move.

11

LOGAN

The stone beneath my hands starts to tremble and... move!

"Oh," Winter gasps next to me.

"What did you do?" I ask.

"Nothing," she says. "I was just leaning, and this piece of rock sunk back."

I grab her face and stamp a kiss on her forehead. "You found the switch!"

Eyes wide and shocked, Winter blinks at me.

I awkwardly let her go, clearing my throat. "Err, yeah. Great work."

I pull back, and we stare in silence as the massive stone slab rises slowly and gently from the floor, sliding upward into a cavity in the rock ceiling.

Beautiful. A simple lever, moved ever so little by pressure at a secret spot, most likely throwing additional weight onto the hidden counter-balances, and causing the monolith to be lifted from the ground.

The search for the mechanism could've taken us ages,

assuming we ever found it, but with Winter's lucky stumble... here we are.

With the door now open, we encounter yet another dark passageway. I don't walk in right away, my excitement so intense I'm petrified on the spot. What lies beyond? Could it really be a secret treasure chamber? What riches will we find? And what if there's nothing? Doesn't matter, Logan, a lost civilization is already the greatest discovery of the century. Like finding a whole new pyramid site no one knew about, not just a mere tomb. Why am I so nervous, then? Because, ah, the possibilities...

"Are we going to check it out or what?"

Smith's prosaic words shake me out of my internal freeze.

"Sure," I say, peering again down the dark passage and then plunging inside.

Following the tunnel for a few yards, we come to an elaborately painted wooden door standing wide open. Whoever was here last either didn't have the time to shut it or forgot to.

"Go on," Smith says impatiently.

Holding my breath, I step through the doorway.

Winter and the soldier press in after me, and we enter a room hewn out of the living rock. On the floor, to the right, a patch of lighter stone catches my eye. The size and shape are that of a big, missing trunk. That, and the wooden door we found ajar, point to an earlier pillaging. One that must've happened centuries ago.

"Hey, Professor," Smith calls. "Point your flashlight this way."

I follow his voice to the opposite side of the chamber, illuminating several large wooden boxes painted gold. About ten by twenty inches in size, they're stacked against the far left wall from the ground up.

"Wow," Winter says, adjusting the headlamp on her forehead

so that it points directly at one box. "What do you think is inside?"

Just as she finishes talking, her light flickers. The device sputters for a few seconds and then goes completely dark.

"Hey." She takes the headlamp off and beats it on her palm to revive it, with no effect. "It's dead!"

"Nothing to worry about," I say. "Mine's working just fine."

We return our attention to the boxes, and I train my light on one at the top and take it down. Even if the room is dry, the lid appears to have rotted over time. Still, a golden lock keeps it secured to the base of the box. I tug at the lock gently, not wanting to break anything, but it doesn't give way.

Smith lets out a sailor's curse and pushes me to the side, saying, "Let me handle it." Before I can stop him, he punches the covering, his fist smashing through the rotten wood.

"Hey!" I protest. "Are you crazy? We need to preserve these boxes; they're artifacts of inestimable value, no matter what they might contain. From now on, you won't touch a single—"

The soldier interrupts my reprimand with a scream of pure joy. "Gold!" Smith plunges his other hand into the box as well and then draws both out full of gold coins that slip through his fingers to go tinkling down to the floor.

I'm momentarily stunned—both by the sight of all that gold, and also by his egregious mistreatment of precious ancient artifacts. Then I regain my wits and shout, "Stop! We will not move anything before it's been properly identified and cataloged. Do I make myself clear?"

"Ah!" Smith says, replacing the coins, "but I have a friend here who begs to disagree with you, Professor."

"What friend?" I say, confused.

The soldier flashes me a grin that sends a cold shiver down

my back, while Winter positions herself next to me, touching my arm from behind.

"Logan," she warns in a low voice.

"See, Professor, Uncle Sam's retirement package isn't as generous as I'd like. I'd be more than happy to round my pension up a little." And then, with a snicker at the boxes, he adds, "Or a lot, if you know what I mean..."

Comprehension finally dawns. "You mean to steal the gold!"

Smith scoffs and cocks his head at Winter, who's hiding behind my shoulder. "A bit slow, isn't he?"

I make to step forward, but Winter holds me back while Smith points his rifle at us.

"Are you for real?" I ask incredulously. "You'll never get away with it."

"We'll see about that," the mercenary says, leering up into my face. "For now, you be a good boy and try not to make my friend" —he pats his M16—"angry. You wouldn't want anything bad to happen to you or the lady."

I'd kill him with my glare if I could, but sadly eye daggers are the only weapons I have. He has me beat, and he knows it.

"Great." Smith nods. "I see we understand each other. Now, shall we explore the rest of the chamber? I'm sure we're all interested in seeing what other treasures it might hold." With the barrel of the rifle, he directs us forward. "You go first, and don't try anything funny."

Still holding the only source of light on top of my head, I walk deeper into the room until I come across a nook about four feet deep and shaped like a bow window. Three stone chests rest below its arch.

Smith comes up beside us. "And what do we have here? Open them," he orders.

I crouch next to the chests and study them. The stone lids

aren't secured by a lock, and when I try to lift the first, it's heavy but it gives. I raise the lid enough to slide it over to the side and lower it to the ground, careful not to let go too quickly so as not to damage it, no matter how much my straining muscles are screaming at me to just drop the damn thing.

Once the top slab is safely on the floor, I lean forward to examine the interior of the chest. But when the light on my head comes into contact with its contents, a silvery sheen dazzles me, blinding me for a second.

"Whoa!" Winter exclaims next to me.

Soon, my eyes grow used to the gleam, and when I peer inside the chest again, I realize with a gasp that it's filled with uncut diamonds, most of them of considerable size.

"Yes!" Smith shouts. "This day keeps getting better and better, doesn't it? I'm going to be the richest man in the world. The black market is getting flooded with diamonds."

The mercenary hunches over and picks up a few, only to let them drop into the chest again.

"You realize you have to carry these through an entire jungle before you can even reach the black market," I say. "With no one catching you."

"You're quite right, Professor," Smith croaks. "But let's first see how many stones we're talking about." He gestures for me to open the other chests.

I begrudgingly follow his orders and set to work pulling the heavy stone lids off the other two chests. Both are filled to the brim with precious gems—not diamonds, but a mix of rubies, emeralds, sapphires...

"Hoorah!" Smith chants and looks about himself. The room has come to a dead end. "Well, then, this is it. Great."

The rogue soldier walks back to the wooden chests of coins and beckons us to follow him.

"Better get to work," he says. "We have what? Sixteen... no, eighteen boxes of gold to move, gems to relocate..." He turns to the patch of lighter stone with a rueful glint in his eyes. "Pity whatever stood there got stolen already." He sighs and shrugs. "All right, let's get started. Give me the light, Professor, and you can begin moving those boxes outside."

I unstrap the headlamp and surrender it before I pick up the first box. It's heavy—must weigh about twenty pounds—but easily transportable.

Smith wiggles the flashlight at Winter. "You, too, Miss Knowles. In the army, we're all for gender equality."

She glares witheringly at him, but the gun in her face leaves her little option but to do as she's told. Winter picks up a box and follows me outside as Smith illuminates the way.

We repeat the journey through the vaulted path nine times. And once all the boxes are stored outside, Smith motions for us to go back inside. When we reach the treasure chamber, he unhooks his backpack from his shoulders and tosses it to Winter.

"Empty it," he orders.

Rather unceremoniously, Winter capsizes the bag, its contents tumbling to the floor: various food provisions, a water canteen, a hunting knife, a lighter, and a first-aid kit. She doesn't spare the objects on the floor a second glance; she's too busy glaring at the colonel. But my eyes immediately fly to the blade, and Smith's malevolent gaze follows mine there.

"Give that a kick, Professor," the soldier says.

I do as he orders, sending the weapon skittering out of my reach.

"Now, Miss Knowles." Smith jerks his chin toward the empty backpack. "If you'd be so kind as to fill the bag with all the gems over there, I'd be terribly grateful."

Winter walks back to the stone chests and, kneeling on the floor, makes a quick job of transferring the precious stones into Smith's backpack. Once she's done, she re-joins me in the center of the room, glaring at the soldier.

"You can stay there and slide the bag toward me," he instructs.

She does, and Smith, keeping his eyes carefully trained on us, bends down and slings the now heavy sack over his shoulders.

"Okay," the colonel says, theatrically pointing the rifle back in our faces. "This has been tremendous fun, but I'm afraid I must leave."

"What?" Winter protests. "You can't mean to leave us locked up in here!"

"Apologies, Miss Knowles, but I must."

"But we're going to die if you trap us in here!"

"Oh, hush, don't be so negative. You have to survive a couple of days—three, tops. I'm sure someone will come and rescue you, eventually."

"Smith, please, you don't have to lock us up," I say. "Tie our hands and leave us outside. Give us a chance."

"Yeah, you're right, Professor, I don't strictly have to ditch you here." The mercenary seems to consider. "I could have you walk outside with me and then find something to tie you to... But this is a huge building, and there's two of you and only one of me. Why risk it? So much simpler to just leave you here..."

"Because we could die!" Winter repeats.

"You have food and water." The colonel points at the floor and at our own backpacks. "You should be fine, unless"—he takes a whiff at the room—"you run out of air." He lets out a bone-chilling laugh. "In which case, I'm really sorry."

He starts backtracking toward the exit, the barrel of his rifle unflinchingly pointed at us.

"Wait," Winter calls desperately. "Aren't you even going to leave us the flashlight?"

"Sorry, miss, kind of need it out there."

We watch him creep away like the poisonous snake he is, the room growing ever darker. Soon he is gone, and we can only hear the stone door closing, all thirty tons of it, slowly pressing down toward the rock below and effectively sealing us in with no means of escape.

12

LOGAN

For a moment, we both stand still, engulfed in the oppressive darkness around us. Buried alive.

No, I refuse to accept that fate. There must be a way out, another secret lever to set the door in motion from within the chamber. But we need to see to search for it.

"Try your flashlight again," I tell Winter.

I hear rustling, and a few seconds later a feeble beam of light cuts through the darkness, illuminating Winter's anxious face.

"Great," I say.

"Great?" she hisses back, her features going from scared to angry. "There's nothing great about our current situation. In case you haven't noticed, we're standing on the wrong side of that nice bit of stone over there. So unless you're hiding a secret stash of dynamite in your backpack, I don't see how we're ever going to get out."

"Don't be so pessimistic. Whoever built this place must have left a switch for the door on the inside—otherwise, they'd risk getting trapped themselves. We just have to find the button

before your lamp goes out again." I point at the flashlight.
"Let's go."

We run down the passage and stop at the door. With
desperate energy, we begin to feel up and down the slab of stone
and the sides of the tunnel. But we find no knob, or contraption,
nor a retracting disk.

"There's nothing here," Winter says in a panicked voice. "It
doesn't work from the inside."

I let my palms roam the bare walls a little longer before I
have to admit defeat.

"Let's go back to the other room and check our supplies,"
I say.

In the treasure chamber, Winter sits behind Smith's leftover
stockpile and balances the headlamp on the floor so that the
light points up in a vertical beam. Then she sorts the food,
looking around herself with a forlorn expression.

"Well," she sighs. "At least our grave will be pretty."

I sit next to her. "Don't be melodramatic. No one's going to
die."

"No? And how do you suppose we're getting out?"

"We came with a team, remember? When we don't return,
they'll come find us."

"What if Smith 'deals' with them the way he dealt with us?"

"Someone will notice the camp has gone silent. Both Dr.
Boonjan and I checked in regularly with the satellite phone, and
Somchai did too to coordinate supply runs with the villagers."

"Even if someone does notice we're missing, they still have to
get to us through the jungle. And then they have to figure out
how to open the secret door! What if they can't? What if they
don't even realize it's there?" Her voice rises a notch. "We're
going to die in here."

She makes some excellent points, but I refuse to give up

hope. We need to stay calm and coherent, and the best way to do that is to busy ourselves with mundane tasks. "We're not going to die," I say firmly. "Now, let's be practical and see where we're at with provisions."

My steadiness seems to calm her down, and we empty both our backpacks and spread everything on the floor. I do a quick assessment. "We have enough food for three or four days, but water is going to become a problem much sooner. We'll have to ration it."

"Splendid," Winter replies sarcastically.

I take a sip from my canteen and encourage Winter to do the same. We share a protein bar, allow ourselves another sip of water, and then I get up to better explore the walls of our prison, in the faint hope of finding some means of escape. But my systematic examination yields no results yet again.

Defeated, I sink to the floor and join Winter in leaning my back against the wall where the gold coin boxes were stashed. Two seconds later, the flashlight begins to flicker again.

"How long have we been in here?" I ask.

Winter shrugs. "A few hours?" She shows me her bare wrist. "I don't have my watch. It was impossible to wear with the scuba-diving gloves."

"Yeah, same here."

The flickering of the headlamp grows more hectic.

"Death by starvation, trapped in a Thai temple," Winter says grimly. "That's not the way I figured I'd go."

"You think of your death often?"

"No, only when I accept stupid jobs, in the stupid jungle, going after stupid lost cities, and oh-so-casually find myself stuck in a stupid treasure chamber," she snaps back.

On that cheerful note, the flashlight blinks one last time and then goes dark.

13

WINTER

I'm so tired, but I can't sleep. Even without the adrenaline flooding through my body—like a trapped animal who stays ready to attack the hunter—the silence alone is too great to allow any rest. Sometimes, I've lain awake at night and thought the quiet oppressive, but it was nothing compared to the perfect stillness of this place. It's as if I could touch the darkness surrounding us.

Everywhere else in the world, a sound or motion, no matter how imperceptible, deadens the sharp edge of absolute silence. But here, there are none.

We're buried in the bowels of a lost temple no one knows about, in a city of legend most don't believe even exists. Outside, the jungle is teeming with life and creatures. The monkeys jumping vines, the exotic birds cooing, the wind rustling through the leaves, but not a sound of it reaches us down here. We're separated by a long tunnel and five feet of rock even from the chamber with the statue of Buddha on his deathbed, and the dead make no sounds. In our living tomb, we're cut off from every echo of the world—as if already in the grave.

I shiver.

"Logan," I whisper. "Would you hold me?"

"Afraid of the dark?" he says.

Why does he have to be such a jerk about everything? "Forget I asked."

A few seconds later, two strong arms drag me to the side. There's some adjusting of limbs, and suddenly I'm engulfed in blissful warmth. Logan has pulled me against his chest and wraps himself around me like a blanket.

Human touch—such a simple thing, but one that can make all the difference in the world.

I let myself relax in Logan's embrace and I'm surprised at how cozy it feels.

"Who are you thinking of?" Logan asks.

I don't hesitate. "My sister. I can't believe I'm going to die without having told her I forgive her. You?"

"For one, I'm not resigned to our demise being such a foregone conclusion." He squeezes his arms around me a little tighter. "And two, there aren't many people for me to think about. I don't have any siblings, and my parents both died a few years back—"

"Oh, I'm sorry."

"Thanks."

"So, you're a bit of a lone wolf?"

"I guess Archie is the closest thing I have to a family now."

"Are you worried Smith will hurt him?"

Logan goes a little rigid behind me. "I don't know... Crazy as Smith is, he didn't seem to want to add a murder charge to his crimes."

"You mean besides our murders?"

"We're not going to die," Logan whispers in my ear. His warm breath brushes down my neck, making me feel the most alive

I've ever been. Funny, since I'm basically lying in a glorified grave.

"You really think a rescue team will get to us in time?"

"Yes," he says.

I choose to believe his lie, and my body lets go of its tension. I shift positions, resting my head back on Logan's shoulder and letting myself go limp in his arms.

I'm already starting to doze off when Logan's hand pats my chest.

What is he doing?

And what gave him the impression he could grope me like that? This might be my last night on Earth, but I sure hope he doesn't expect me to put out just because of that.

Oh crap, why did I ask him to hug me? Did I give him the wrong idea? Now what do I do?

My first reaction is to swat his hand away and go back to sitting in my corner, but my body refuses to do my brain's bidding. And what if this really turns out to be my last night in this world? Would spending it having sex with a gorgeous man really be the worst way to go? It's certainly better than sitting alone in the cold.

And since when do we think Logan is gorgeous? a little voice asks in my head.

Oh, please, we've always thought that. Only he made it an easy trait to ignore by behaving like Satan. But since he's started to act kind of nice, it's become harder to overlook.

He pats me again, missing my breasts by a mile. Should I give him pointers? Is this his idea of foreplay? Should I—

"Is this your camera?" Logan interrupts my train of thought.

Gosh, he's bad at foreplay. "Mm-hmm?"

"Does it have any battery left?"

"Yeah, almost full, why?"

"I've been thinking about something Smith said before locking us in here."

Smith?!

I guess hot, last-night-on-Earth sex wasn't on his mind after all.

"What?" I ask.

"He said we'd be rescued sooner or later, unless we ran out of oxygen first. That's got me thinking... We've been stuck for hours, but the air hasn't grown hot or stale."

I take a deep breath. "No, it hasn't," I agree. "This room isn't that big—we would have noticed the lack of oxygen by now."

"Exactly. Which means fresh air has to come in from some-where. It makes sense, otherwise, we should've been stifled or poisoned when we first came in. But the air felt totally normal—no toxins or anything from sitting still and stale over centuries. That big stone door looked air-tight, so the inlet must be some-where else." He squeezes my wrist in excitement. "And if the air can come in, maybe we can squeeze out from the same place. We only need to find the spot."

"We've searched everywhere already."

"So? Maybe we missed something. It's worth giving it another go. Can we use the flash of your camera to light the way?"

"Mmm, the flash is really battery-consuming... Maybe the screen backlight is enough?" I fumble with the camera's buttons to switch it on.

When it does, I turn and find Logan smiling down at me.

He gives me a strong, squeezing hug and kisses the side of my head. "If we get out of here alive, I swear I'm never going to complain about you taking my picture ever again."

I mock scold him with a deep frown, and we both get up.

For an hour or more, we go on feeling about the chamber,

looking not for secret buttons this time, but for a crack where the air might be getting in. We start standing, then end up on our hands and knees to cover the lower section of the walls. Logan scrutinizes every square inch of space while I hold the camera screen at eye level.

I'm beginning to despair when Logan suddenly says, "Feel here."

I lower my reflex to the floor. "Where?"

"Put your hand over mine. Do you feel anything?"

A tendril of electricity shoots up my arm from where our skin is touching, but I bet "a current shock" is not what Logan means me to feel.

"I think there's air coming up," he continues. "Listen."

Logan rises and stamps his foot down, and a flame of hope shoots up in my heart when it rings hollow. We're in the far corner of the chamber, which explains why we hadn't noticed the echoing sound during our former exhaustive examination.

"Can you make the screen any brighter?" Logan asks.

I comply with his request; I was keeping it on low to save power, but if there's a way out that's no longer necessary. Even at maximum brightness, though, the screen's light is not the best as we scrutinize the spot like two angry hawks. There's nothing here.

I'm losing hope again when I see it: a crease in the solid rock floor. And... yes! It's covered in so much dust, it's barely recognizable, but I still spot it: a stone ring! Could it be the handle to a secret escape door?

Logan must spot it at the same time as me, because he gasps.

We look at each other, saying no words. We're too excited; or, at least, I am. My heart is beating too wildly with hope to allow me to speak.

"I need Smith's knife," Logan says, and scrambles back to where our little mound of provisions is lying abandoned.

He comes back with the knife and scratches around the ring with it. Finally, he manages to work it under and lifts the stone hoop away—gently, for fear of breaking the hook. Being made of stone, it hasn't rusted in all the centuries it has lain there, as would have been the case had it been made of iron. Logan pushes the ring up until it's standing upright. Then he thrusts his hands into it and tugs with all his force... but nothing budges.

"Let me try," I say impatiently.

Logan shakes his head but lets me have a go. Maybe if I come at it from a different angle... I pull on the damn thing for dear life, but nothing, it doesn't give.

The blasted thing is wedged right in the corner, so the walls make it impossible for both of us to pull at once.

Logan tries and fails again. He swipes his forehead with his shirt sleeve and sinks back into a crouch, thinking. He grabs the knife again and begins scratching all around the crack where we felt the air coming up.

Next, he takes his shirt off and runs it through the ring, tying it in place with a tight knot.

And I know this is a life and death situation, but damn! The professor is ripped. Not that I didn't know that, of course, but now, staring at his strong back and chest, both covered in a light sheen of perspiration, I can't help my mouth watering a little.

Logan sets his feet firmly on the floor, one in front of the other in a wide stance, then ropes the shirt around his forearm and pulls, offering me an even more detailed view of all the muscles ripping his torso.

"I need your help," he says in a strained voice. "Get in front of me and pull with all you've got."

Oh, right, that might be more useful than standing here ogling!

I do as he says, molding my body to his. We're back to chest, and all this proximity is making me hot, and... I need to focus! Let's get out of the grave first, and then I can reflect on why Logan is suddenly pushing all my lust buttons. I grab the shirt with both hands and pull, pull, pull until my hands hurt and the fabric of the shirt starts to rip in my grip.

"Keep going," Logan encourages me. "It's giving!" he gasps.

Suddenly, there's a grating sound, then a rush of air, and then we're on the floor. I land on top of Logan as the heavy flagstone slides away to reveal a dark opening.

"We did it!" I yell, and turn to smile at Logan.

Only now I'm awkwardly straddling him while my hands are firmly placed on his bare pecs, and is it just me or is he looking at me funny? I quickly climb off him, pick myself up, and inhale a long breath.

Logan does the same, and we both stare at the spot where the stone was, which now reveals the first step of a stone stair.

"What now?" I ask.

"Let's gather our things," Logan says. "We don't know what might await us down there."

We quickly collect our belongings, dividing them evenly between our two backpacks. And, to my dismay, Logan puts his shirt back on... only to find it hangs around his chest in tatters, leaving me a clear view of his six-pack.

Small victories.

Logan shakes his head and ties a few strands together.

"Are you going for the fifties-housewife look?" I tease.

"Right now, any look is better than corpse-in-a-chamber, wouldn't you agree?" he says, and smiles at me.

A real, megawatt smile. One that transforms his entire face, brightens it even in the semi-darkness, and—oh gosh! I seriously need to rein in the lust.

Or scratch the itch! the evil little voice in my head suggests.

Yeah, right. As if.

I internally shake my head at the possibility and look at the hole in the floor. "So we just follow the stairs?"

"Of course," Logan says, and picks up the camera-turned-flashlight. "I'll go first."

"Careful where you put your feet," I say. "I don't want you to fall down and break your neck."

Logan's answering grin is wolfish. "Wow, worried about my safety now? I'm touched." He puts a mocking hand over his heart.

"Annoying as you are." I scowl. "I'd still rather not be left down here alone."

"Yeah," Logan says, his predatory grin shifting into something softer. "You're growing on me, too. Let's go?"

I didn't say he was growing on me—Oh, wait. I'm growing on him? Was he serious?

I don't have time to dwell on the answer, as Logan is already descending the first step of the stone stairs.

I follow him and, by the time we've reached the bottom, I've counted thirty steps.

"Decision time," Logan says, stopping.

The dim glow of the screen illuminates a T-intersection, with narrow tunnels running off in both directions. Logan stands in the middle of the new passage, very still.

"What are you doing?" I ask.

"Trying to decide if we should go left or right?"

I scrunch my face, perplexed. "How?"

The way I see it, it's just bare walls. With no sign whatsoever which direction will lead to safety and which to a horrible death trapped in the bowels of this temple.

"I'm trying to gauge which way the draft is coming from."

"Any luck?"

"No, it's too faint. Wait!" He hands me the camera, then rummages in his backpack and pulls out a lighter.

"We had a lighter this whole time?" I ask. I hadn't noticed one upstairs. "Why didn't you use it in the chamber?"

"First, I was worried about burning up what oxygen we had, and then we used your camera, so..."

Logan flicks the lighter to life. At once, the flame blows to the left.

"That way," Logan announces, pointing to the right. He pockets the lighter and takes the reflex back. "We have to go against the draft. Air draws inwards, not outwards."

The words have barely left his mouth when the camera in his hands goes dark, the battery dead at last. Blackness surrounds us once again.

"Use the lighter," I say.

Logan turns it back on, and in the flickering light, I see that he has looped my camera around his neck.

"Let's go," he prompts me. But, as soon as he takes a step forward, he stops and blows out the flame. "I can't walk with the lighter in my hands. The flame blows backward and burns my fingers."

"So what do we do?"

"We'll have to grope our way forward and hope this blasted tunnel is short." I'm about to protest when Logan, probably sensing my discomfort, adds, "Hold my hand."

One hand safely tucked into his, I feel along the wall with the other and walk along, trying the ground before me at every step.

After about half an hour, the passage suddenly takes a sharp turn. We flick on the lighter again to make sure there aren't any off-shoot passages, then head onward. After a while, there's another turn, then another, until I lose count and am utterly disoriented. I have no idea which direction we're going, or how much time has passed since we lost the camera light, but I'm losing hope we'll ever get out of here alive. We're buried in a stone maze that doesn't lead anywhere. Hell, maybe we're going in circles. Whoever built this place probably thought it'd be a fun joke to give us hope of escaping, only to trap us in a much worse nightmare.

"Logan," I say. "I need a break."

We stop and use the lighter to fish two protein bars out of the backpacks and eat them in the flickering light of the small flame.

Not exactly my idea of a candlelit dinner, or breakfast, or whatever this is. I have no idea what time it is, or if it's still today or already tomorrow. Day, night... I just don't know. I need to get out of here or I might go crazy.

"Ready to go on?" Logan asks, once we've drunk the last of our water.

I nod.

He offers me his hand once again and snuffs the lighter.

We trudge on, nothing changing in our surroundings for what feels like hours. Until, over the rustling of our feet on the ground, I catch a sound. Very faint and very far off, but definitely a noise. A distant murmuring of...

"Logan," I say, pulling on his hand to make him stop. "Do you hear it?"

We pause, holding our breath and straining our ears.

"I do."

"What is it?"

"Sounds like running water." I hear the smile in Logan's answer. "Let's go; we can't be too far off."

Summoning the last of our energy, we grope our way along the rocky walls, the sound becoming more and more audible. We go on and on until we can distinctly make out the unmistakable swirl of rushing water.

"You think it's an underground river?" I ask.

"It must be," Logan says. "I swear I can smell the water —Aaah..."

Splash!

A sudden tug on my hand makes me tumble forward, and I follow Logan down, sinking headfirst into the river below. Even in the initial moment of surprise, I manage not to let go of Logan's hand. I quickly recover from the shock of the fall and start kicking my feet to keep my head above water toward where Logan is pulling me.

He must find some kind of hold, because all of a sudden we stop floating with the current, and his hand keeps me anchored in place.

"Are you all right?" he asks.

"Yeah, you?"

"Yep, but we need to get out of the water. I think I can pull myself out and then drag you up." He places my hand on the protruding boulder of rock he's clinging to. "Hold on to this."

I hear more splashing noises and feel Logan's body slither past mine like a giant eel. Once he's safely on solid ground, two strong arms I'm becoming too familiar with descend on me and pull me up.

Shivering, I ask, "What do we do now?"

"We must follow the river; it's our best bet to get out."

"Okay, but let's use the lighter, I can hold it and flick it on from time to time. I'm not looking forward to another freezing bath."

I hear Logan's movements as he searches for it and tries to turn it on. "It's not lighting up."

"What do we do now?"

"We still have to follow the river."

"What? In the darkness? How are we not going to fall in again?"

"I think it's safer than trying to swim our way out. We'll go slowly. I'm sure we can make it."

And just when I thought the situation couldn't get any worse, I discover that being soaked head to toe definitely isn't an improvement. As we start down the tunnel again, we both drip unpleasantly, making the way even more slippery and treacherous.

Slowly, utterly exhausted, we stumble ahead for what seems forever, but could be only minutes.

Suddenly Logan stops, and I bump against him.

"Look!" he whispers. "Am I starting to have visions, or is that light?"

I strain my eyes, squinting in the darkness... and, yes, far ahead of us, I can definitely make out a faint, glimmering spot, no larger than a cottage windowpane. It's so dim and distant, that I, too, doubt my sight. I close my eyes and open them again, but the dot is still there. Very much real.

Squeezing Logan's hand, I say, "I can see it too!"

With a gasp of hope, we push on. In five minutes, there's no longer any doubt; it's a patch of light, becoming larger with every step we take. A minute more, and a breath of living air fans on us. We struggle on, now keeping to the left, as close to the tunnel wall and away from the running water as we can. It becomes easier as we go on and the passage expands.

A few more steps and we're out in the sun again.

14

LOGAN

After so many hours trapped in that tomb, the first gulp of fresh air that fills my lungs is the sweetest I've ever tasted. I turn to find Winter beaming up at me in the faint light of the approaching dawn. She's wet as a drowned rat, smeared all over with dust and mud, bruised, the fear of certain death still visible in her eyes. And yet, I've never seen a more beautiful woman in my entire life.

I smile back at her. "We made it!"

Winter surprises me with a high-five, and then undoes her tresses and shakes the water off, wet-dog style. I'm positively hypnotized.

"Where are we?" she asks.

I check our surroundings, trying to orient myself. We're on a hill, the mass of the temple at our backs, and a stretch of untouched jungle expanding before us in a huge valley.

"We must've gotten out the other side of the temple," I say, taking a better look at the vale opening below us.

That's when my brain clicks.

The memory of the satellite images superimposes with the

planes and hills before my eyes, turning rises into buildings and the flat stretches of ground into roads and plazas.

"Look," I say, pointing forward. "This isn't natural. See the straight lines and regularity of the mounds?"

I can't believe it! It's like staring at a monochromatic-green plastic of a city grid. There are roads, canals, and moats around all the principal structures, and the river we followed must be an artificial stream; it encloses and encircles the city. All the important buildings face east, toward the rising sun, as was often the case in local ancient cultures. The temple we came out of does, and so do the other vine-covered mounds— which are probably the city's religious and government buildings.

At the city's edge, forts and walls line the perimeter, and underneath the vegetation, I can see sparkles of gold in the dawn's light. An entire city of gold—and I don't care if it's just a layer of paint. Once cleaned of the weeds, this will be the most magnificent historical site in the world.

Winter steps next to me. "It's really something, huh? Pity you drowned my camera. This would've been a beautiful picture."

Is she seriously blaming me for the camera? It's not like I tried to fall into the river. "Sorry if I was busy trying to save both our lives," I snap.

She nudges me gently with her elbow. "I was kidding."

"Oh."

Winter runs her fingers between her wet locks, distracting me from my irritation. "What's the plan now?" she asks. "Where do you reckon Smith's at?"

"Judging from the sun's position, we must've been trapped in the temple for about twelve hours. I bet Smith used this time to move the boxes out of the building, but he can't carry the booty away by himself. He must plan to use the mule, and Somchai took it back to base camp. If we're lucky, he's waiting at the temporary camp for them to return."

"And then what?" Winter asks. "He single-handedly takes everyone out and escapes?"

"Nah, Carter or Montgomery will be in the group, and those two do everything Smith tells them. They're professional fighters with weapons, and even if they're outnumbered, they can over-power the others in a blink."

"Okay, then we need to take Smith out before they arrive."

"Why?"

"Because he thinks we're still trapped in the temple. With the element of surprise, we might stand a chance against one armed ex-Delta Force, but there's no way we can take down two. Surprise or not."

"And how do you plan to take out Smith?"

"Easy. We steal his rifle."

"Sorry, but that would be useless; I can't shoot."

Winter flashes me a wicked smile and slowly walks toward me. "You may not, Doctor." She stops a foot away from me and gently pokes me in the chest. Then, with a wink, she adds, "But I sure can."

* * *

One hour later, we've circled our way back to the front of the temple and have eyes on our temporary camp. The place is abso-lutely still, which hopefully means Smith is still asleep in his tent. But his M16 is nowhere to be seen.

"No rifle," I whisper.

"Well," Winter whispers back, "if I were a crook sleeping alone in the jungle, I'd take the big guns to bed with me."

"So what do we do?"

"Cover me," she says. "I'll sneak inside his tent and steal it."

"And how am I supposed to cover you?"

"I don't know." Winter shrugs. "Grab a shovel. If Sleeping Beauty wakes up, smash it on his head, I don't care. He had it coming."

Gingerly, careful not to make too much noise, we approach Smith's tent. But when Winter pulls the flap open, the inside is empty. Well, not exactly empty. The rifle is there, but Smith isn't.

With a quick precision that's half hot, half scary, Winter grabs Smith's M16, checks it for ammunition, and then cocks it over her shoulder. A rustling sound coming from behind makes us turn, and before I've had time to realize what's happening, Winter bursts through the tent flap, trains the rifle on Smith, and shouts, "Stop right there! Hands up where I can see them."

At the edge of the jungle, Smith, probably back from taking a leak, freezes with his hands in the air. His ever-present leer is not one bit dimmed by suddenly finding himself on the wrong side of the weapon.

"Come on, Barbie," the soldier snickers. "We both know that rifle is useless in those pretty hands of yours—"

He reaches for the gun at his belt, but Winter is quicker, and sends a bullet flying an inch from Smith's foot. Dirt explodes in a circular bubble near his toes, and Smith backs his hand away from his gun.

Eyes fixed on the rifle sight, she says, "Try a move like that again, and the next bullet goes in your kneecap."

Again, I don't know if I should be turned on or frightened to death.

"Oi, Barbie can shoot." The soldier chuckles mockingly. "The world is full of surprises. I confess I hadn't hoped to see you again so soon, Miss Knowles."

"What can I say," Winter quips right back. "I was missing you too much. Now, would you be so kind as to remove that gun from your belt, and the one at your ankle. The knives, too. Go slowly, and not another funny move."

Some sort of unspoken sniper secret code must run between them, because to my utter surprise, Smith does exactly as he's told. He must have finally decided Winter is a threat.

Once the colonel has removed all the weapons from his person, Winter instructs him to kick them our way. He does, and I quickly collect them, still eyeing my companion skeptically.

"How come you're such a good shot?" I ask.

Her eyes flicker to me for a fraction of a second, and she smirks. "My mom's from Indiana, originally." She refocuses on Smith. "She was born and raised on a ranch, and we went to visit our grandparents every summer. Pops taught us how to shoot before we could walk."

I swallow. "Remind me to never make you angry again."

"Oh, I will." She gives me that sweet, bone-chilling smile of hers, and then her face loses all humor. "Logan," Winter says, her voice hard as steel. "We need to find a wire or something we can tie him with. I can't keep him at gunpoint forever."

I check the supplies Somchai left us and come back with two lengths of rope.

"Throw one at him," Winter instructs.

I frown. "Why?"

"So he can tie his own feet."

"I can do it," I offer.

"No, you can't," Winter says. "He could grab you in a hundred different ways the second he gets his hands on you and threaten to choke you or snap your neck. Our government paid top dollars to transform him into a living killing machine. We're both staying well away from him until he's incapacitated."

Smith's responding sneer is evil. "Other than being a good

shot, you're smarter than I thought," he says, something close to admiration audible in his voice.

I throw him the rope, and Smith obediently ties his feet together. I'll make sure to check that the knots are tight once his hands are bound.

Winter gives him her next order. "Now tie the other rope around your wrist, bring your hands to your back, and loop the rope inside your belt twice. Then turn around—as always, slowly."

Smith does, and when he has one hand securely restrained behind him, Winter says, "Logan, time to finish the job."

I tie his other hand, then lift the colonel bodily, drag him to a nearby tree, and use the rope to secure him to the trunk.

Once Smith is restrained, and I've double-checked the knots, Winter lowers the rifle, letting her shoulders relax.

"What's next, G.I. Jane?" I ask. "Should we wait for the rest of the group?"

"No, we make a run for it."

"Why? We have him. There's no more danger of—"

"Carter or Montgomery will arrive soon. They might just blunder in and get the jump on us, or they might scout ahead, see Smith tied up, and ambush us. Too many things could go wrong. We need to get lost, find civilization, and call for help."

"You expect me to leave him here? With all the gold? So he and his cronies can steal it?"

"I don't care about the stupid treasure; I just want to make it out of the jungle alive. We have to find help."

"And what of the others? We need to warn them."

"We can't; Logan, we have to go. Every second we lose is thinning our chances."

"Listen to Barbie, Professor," Smith taunts. "Make yourselves scarce and hope we don't catch you."

Winter scowls at him but doesn't engage. "Let's gather what we can and get out of here."

First, we take our fill of water from the stock Somchai left behind. After a day and a night spent rationing, the water is sweet and fresh as it flows down my parched throat. I gulp it down until my stomach begins to stretch. Then I fill all the canteens I'm comfortable carrying, and, finally, reload my back-pack with more food. Lastly, I pick up one of the machetes. I'd like to take them all, but they'd be too heavy to bear. Winter, her hair now dry, combs it back in her signature twin braids, gathers her camera gear, and nods at me that she's ready.

"Which way should we go?" I ask.

Throwing a hateful glare at Smith, she comes next to me to whisper in my ear. "Let's retrace our steps on the road for a while, then we can decide. Should make it harder for them to track us."

"Okay. Somchai and the others shouldn't arrive before noon, which should give us a good head start."

"All right."

We nod at each other and, without sparing Smith another glance, we head for the thick of the jungle.

"Au revoir," the soldier calls mockingly after us, just as dark, heavy storm clouds obscure the sky and a clap of thunder rumbles in the distance.

15

WINTER

Of course we have to make our escape under an avalanche of water. And, in the Thai jungle, it doesn't just rain buckets—we're flooded by so much rainwater, it's as if someone opened the sky's tap and is in no hurry to close it.

By now, I should've learned any situation can get worse, and that, lately, being soaked in water is what does the trick. Why did I ever complain about the heat? Compared to the wet cold sneaking down my spine, the excessive warmth of two days ago was heaven.

At the moment, I'm drenched, shirt to socks, and my boots are caked in mud. With every new step, I half expect my feet to fall off from their weight.

Suddenly, the ground beneath me gives way, swallowing me whole. A scream rolls out of my throat as, head over heels, I topple over the landslide, rocks, muck, and rubble falling in a waterfall around me.

I lose the rifle in the plunge, but I'm kind of glad. The last thing I need is a pointy slab of metal batting all over me as I fall.

Did I put the safety on? I can't remember. It'd be ironic if I got shot by Smith's stolen M16 by accident.

As I careen around a bend, Logan rolls past me, making a good impression of a bob racer without a sleigh. Hell, that's where we're headed. Satan is taking me home with him: to the pitch-dark bottom of this inferno of a jungle. Having been trapped in the bowels of the earth wasn't enough. Oh, no. Now I'm sinking into an abyss where only mud and torn branches exist.

A runaway boulder smashes into my elbow as it rolls past. As I keep tumbling, I bring my arm closer to my chest. I don't think it's broken, but it stings worse than a scorpion bite. With my other hand, I claw at the hill, hoping to find some kind of anchor to stop my downward plunge, but my fingernails scrape the earth in vain. I'm plummeting too fast for me to hold on to anything. Like in a nightmare from my childhood, when I slipped off a rafting boat in West Virginia to be immediately carried under by a powerful current with no hope of rescue. Only, I'm not lost in the rapids today, but in a sea of mud. I'll end up being buried alive, again!

My clothes rip in multiple places as thorns and sharp rocks slash at the fabric. I cover my face to prevent more dirt from entering my mouth, and close up in a tight ball, steering sideways to take most of the slide on my back, where the backpack protects my skin. But it's no use. My ribs hit something, throwing me off balance, and the next moment I find myself on my stomach, legs flung behind me.

I am on the brink of losing it, but I refuse to let myself succumb to blind panic. I can't control where my body is going, but I can still rule my thoughts. We didn't escape a stone tomb just to plunge into a dirt grave. I cool my mind, focusing on all the people I love and want to get back to: my parents, Summer,

Lana, the rest of our team—they need us. I repeat their names in my head, my love for them working as a shield protecting my body against the pain of the rockslide. Until, with a dull crunch, I slam into the bottom of the cliff, my limbs exploding into a starburst of pain.

An instant later, Logan tumbles over me, the rifle bouncing down right after him and missing both our heads by inches.

"Whooo-hoo!" Logan hollers, rolling off me. "Heck of a ride. Are you okay?"

Heavy raindrops smack my face, washing the mud away. "I think so," I say, swallowing a mouthful of rain. "I'm still in one piece."

The adrenaline from the fall must jack up my system, because I feel no pain. Only the rain rinsing the dirt out of my braids and shredded clothes.

"You?" I ask.

"Only a few scratches," Logan says with a big grin. Then he offers me a hand. "Come on, we gotta press the advantage. We don't know how long we have before Smith gets free, and you can bet he'll be onto us again soon."

I let him pull me up and lose my breath as our faces come within inches of each other. All I'd have to do to kiss him would be to rise up on tiptoes.

Whoa.

Whoa. Whoa. Whoa.

Where did that thought come from?

All these life-threatening experiences are playing funny games with my brain.

And his, too, judging from the way his green-hazel eyes darken as he looks at me. As if he, too, was thinking about kissing me.

Thunder cracks in the distance, sounding disturbingly like a gunshot. The sudden noise pulls us both back to our senses, to the urgency of the situation and away from any crazy romantic fantasies.

I step back and scan our surroundings. We landed in a small clearing, but except for the spot we're standing in, the terrain is still jungle all around. "Which direction?" I ask.

"Depends where we want to go."

"We have options?"

Logan considers for a second. "I see only two choices: either we try for the village or walk back to camp."

"The village would be safer, but it's farther away." I gnaw my bottom lip and twist my fingers. "And I don't feel right not checking on the others."

"Same here."

"What do you think Smith plans to do to them?"

"Best case, he ties them up and he and his minions leave with the booty."

"Worst case?"

Logan shrugs. "Hard to say. He left us sealed in a tomb to die. Kind of a big tell on the guy's character."

"But you said he wasn't a murderer," I protest, recovering the rifle. Smith's M16 is muddy but seems otherwise undamaged. I check to make sure the safety's on, then look down the barrel. It's unclogged, shouldn't be jammed.

Logan smiles apologetically. "I was only trying to comfort you."

I knew he was lying. I don't know if I should be mad or grateful. The lie did make me feel better at a time when I desperately needed comfort, so I land on grateful.

"Then we have to check the camp," I say, making the decision. "Let's make sure our friends are okay, and then we'll see from there."

"All right."

I turn in a half-circle. I have no idea where we are. "Which way?"

Logan closes his eyes.

"Err?" I cough. "Are you trying to meditate the answer?"

He frowns, but keeps his lids closed. "I'm picturing a mental map of the area."

After a few minutes, he blinks and stares up at the sky.

"Any luck?" I ask.

Logan stalks over to the edge of the vegetation. "Our best bet is to head west and then south, circle back the opposite way we came."

"And how can you tell where the west is?"

He pulls the machete out from the sheath on his belt and points it at the sky. The rain has finally abated, turning into a drizzle while the clouds are clearing away. "The sun's moving that way. We should follow."

* * *

Logan

After ten days in the jungle, my muscles are used to the strain of handling a machete. But trained or not, I'm tiring fast. I haven't slept in I don't know how many hours, I've only eaten two protein bars in as much time, and there's no one to rotate with. The heat doesn't help either. The sun is up and shining again and it has turned the jungle into an open-air Turkish bath. So, even if the forest is less thick down here, we're slow. Too slow.

If we keep this snail's pace, I'm afraid the soldiers will catch up with us soon.

As if on cue, three bullets rip into the trees directly in front of me, saving me the need to use the machete. I dive sideways and careen into Winter, taking her down with me. We find cover behind a boulder, her soft curves pressed up against me, and I spare a second to catch my breath before peeking over the rim of the rock.

Smith and his cronies are standing at the edge of the cliff, having easily spotted us from the high ground. Another round of shots rings through the air, and bullets zing against the boulder. I duck behind the stone again.

"Smith?" Winter asks.

"Yeah, and he brought his merry band of mercenaries."

"Both Carter and Montgomery? How come they're both with him?"

I shrug. "How am I supposed to know?"

"We need to get out of here. We're sitting ducks without the cover of the jungle."

I rub my forehead, my head splitting with a headache. "In case you haven't noticed, I'm exhausted, and cutting down vines isn't an easy-peasy job."

She pats the machete at her side. "I can help."

"No, you can't. You're not strong enough."

"Why do you always have to assume—"

I point at a thick root at her feet. "Cut that," I interrupt. I don't have time for a feminist protest. This isn't about her being a woman.

Winter unleashes the machete from her belt and swings it at the root. The blade barely makes a dent before it harmlessly slides off to the side.

I raise my machete and, with one clean slash, I split the root in the middle.

Winter's glare subsides. "I see your point."

Even though the situation is dire, I find it in me to grin. "Careful there, that almost sounded as if you were admitting I was right and you were wrong."

She smiles back and jokingly pokes me. "Never."

More bullets make the vegetation around us splinter, sobering us up.

If only I could see what they're doing, but they're so far away. Then an idea strikes me. "Do you have anything in your photographic equipment I could use as a binocular?"

Winter unslings the backpack from her shoulders and rummages inside for a few seconds. She hands me a contraption that looks like a miniature telescope. "Try this."

I bring it to my eye, but another round of bullets prevents me from looking.

I don't notice that Winter also took her camera out of the backpack until she's raised her head out of cover, prompting a fresh bout of gunfire. Shards of rock fly in all directions.

"Are you crazy?" I grab Winter by the collar of her shirt and drag her back down. "What are you doing?"

"Collecting evidence. The police will need proof. Otherwise, it's our word against theirs."

"Not if you get your head blown off. Put that camera away and focus on staying alive."

Begrudgingly, she does as I say.

Then I notice everything has gone quiet. I bring the mini telescope to my eyes, wrestle with the zoom to focus the lens, and chance a look.

"Damn! They're dropping ropes over the side of the cliff." I watch as one by one they rappel their way down, Smith in the lead. "They're coming." I turn to Winter. "On my three, we jump out and make a run for it." She nods, and so I start the count-down. "One, two... three!"

We jump to our feet and dash forward, leaving the clearing behind. Just as we plunge into the cover of the jungle, a rain of bullets pelts the stretch of earth we were standing on only seconds ago.

As we charge through the trees, branches slap against my face. The growth is too dense for me to duck out of the way. Winter is having an even worse time than me. I check on her as we run and see her struggle as one of her braids gets caught in a low branch. Hands flying to her head, she yanks at it and struggles free, but not without leaving a long blond lock entangled in the prickly vine.

The undergrowth becomes denser. Machete in hand, I hack as fast as I can, fresh adrenaline giving me the strength I lacked before. Cursing under my breath, I slash at the vines and tree limbs with clean strokes of the blade, clearing a narrow passage. My muscles scream in protest from the effort, but fear spurs me on, fueling my arm as it whips through the underbrush at light-ning speed. Let's hope Smith and his mercenaries aren't good trackers. Our only chance is to lose them.

Winter stumbles behind me, but I can't spare the energy to check on her; I'm too busy battling the palms. Salty sweat pours down my face and arms, turning the million cuts and scratches on my skin into as many tiny flaming welts. But, despite the knotted, aching muscles and constant tension in my arms, my sole focus is on keeping my machete arm going.

My grip on the handle has become almost maniacal; I don't dare to flex my fingers for fear of dropping the blade, regardless of the cramping. Handle fused to my palm, I develop a rhythm in a life-or-death dance with the vegetation as my partner. Arm up, I aim for oblique cuts, followed by a backhand hack when I don't finish the job on the first try, and a strong pull from my free hand to clear the chopped branches. Raise, cut, chop, pull. Raise, cut, chop, pull. Over and over again until my arm becomes one with the machete.

Every swipe is crucial. I can't afford even a single miss, as every inch I carve forward keeps us alive. I try not to think of the consequences should Smith overtake us. There won't be any prisoners this time around. Smith isn't a fool-me-twice kind of fella.

At my heels, Winter isn't faring any better. Each time she staggers or gets slapped by a branch, she gasps and lets out a quick breath.

"How are you holding up?" I say, glancing back at her.

"This rifle is too heavy," she pants. "I'm dropping it."

"What?" I yell, all the while hacking away at the jungle. "You can't drop our only weapon. Leave the backpack."

"No way, I have all my equipment in here."

"And how are a bunch of cameras going to help us stay alive?" I turn just a fraction to glare at her. "Are you going to photograph Smith to death?"

"I'm not leaving my cameras behind; do you have any idea how much they cost? You've already wrecked one."

"Here." I pause for a second and backtrack to her. I snatch the rifle from her hands and sling it over my shoulders.

The short break is enough for men's voices to carry over to us, the ring of their whizzing machetes audible now that mine has stopped. Smith and his men are moving in closer. I redouble my efforts, slicing into the undergrowth—raise, cut, chop, pull, raise, cut, chop, pull—while sweat pours down my face and spine.

Another palm falls, and we reach a less dense stretch of jungle. I grab Winter's hand and we take off at a run.

I glance over my shoulder and catch glints of silver flashing through the thick greenery. They sweep up and down in identical semicircles, their eerie ring whizzing through the air. Too much silver for three men; the soldiers must be spinning a blade in each hand, gaining on us even faster.

As the sound of the machetes grows louder, I wipe sweat from my eyes with my shirt sleeve, stumble, and waste precious seconds. I get up and race on. A dense thicket gets in my way, so I slice at it with more aggressive swings and push forward. And almost drop eighty feet into the violently churning river below.

I fling my arms out just in time to stop Winter from tumbling over the edge, and we stare in horror at the jagged sides of the cliff covered in thick, gnarled vines. We're trapped!

"Look," Winter says, pointing to our right. "There's a bridge."

Hope swells in my chest, only to be crushed when I spot the crumbling wooden structure she's referring to. The "bridge" is a narrow, broken-down assemblage of rotting planks covered in vines and dangling precariously over the void. Even when newly constructed, I bet it couldn't hold two people abreast, and mustn't have had the strength to carry more than ten in total. And in the present, I fear a single person would be too much. The wood has been ravaged by hundreds of years of exposure to the elements: rain, wind, sun, and whatever else this hideous jungle has thrown at it. That is, where there's any wood left. Many of the bridge's boards are missing or shattered in half.

"That's not a bridge," I say, unhooking the rifle from my shoulder, ready to make my final stand. "That's a historical artifact."

"Oh, please," Winter scoffs as I kneel behind a tree trunk, trying to spot the exact position of Smith and his sergeants. "You can't even shoot."

"I'm a quick study," I say, pulling a lever I hope removes the safety. How hard can it be? Point and shoot, right?

"I'm taking my chances with the bridge," Winter says.

The first plank groans under her weight as she steps on it, but I don't turn to witness the stubborn woman's walk to her certain death. I focus on the jungle, trying to pinpoint the exact location of our pursuers. They seem to be coming from the left, where I can hear the rustling of the vegetation being trashed and trampled. Let's see if I retained some marksmanship from my childhood days playing at cowboys with air guns. My only chance is to quickly pick the soldiers off before they overtake us.

I aim the M16 toward the advancing militia, and only detach my eyes from the rifle sight to spare a glance at Winter. She's made it a third of the way across the bridge, but I bet she can't make it halfway before the whole thing comes crashing down. The photographer will fall and smash her pretty head on the craggy rocks below, and her limp body will be swept away by the fast-moving waters before I can look. Already, the boards she's passing are tearing off and scurrying down into the river where they are mutilated on impact.

"Come back!" I yell. "That's suicide."

My call is answered by the hiss of bullets hitting wood a few feet left of my position. A blind attack. I peek over the trunk and, just as blindly, try to return the fire. I raise the rifle, pull the trigger, but nothing happens.

How do I remove the damn safety? I'm uselessly pawing at the rifle when suddenly... snap! I turn just in time to panic as the board under Winter's feet gives way and spirals down into the river. Showing quick reflexes, she grabs onto the railing, managing to keep a hold of the fraying rope. Through the rips in her shirt, I can see the muscles in her arms tense with the effort of pulling herself up. Once she's standing again, Winter keeps her feet at the base of the railing and with quick sidesteps, hoists herself to the other side of the canyon. She leaps over the last ruined section of the bridge, landing safely on a bed of ferns.

A bullet zings past my ear, informing me I'm quickly running out of options. Ah, hell! If she can make it across... I'll just have to be faster in my crossing. I stop fighting with the rifle and sling it back over my shoulder, tightening the strap. With a few quick strides, I'm at the bridgehead, already pulling on a vine to test it. Another strong tug, and I declare it safe. I backtrack a few steps to create a runway of sorts before I make the leap. But just as I take the first step, the vine goes limp in my hands.

I drop the useless piece of vegetation and glance backward over my shoulder. A groan escapes my lips as I spot a silver blade not thirty feet away. They're almost here. This is it, then. I can only choose if I want to die splattered on the riverbank, or with a bullet in my back. I'll take my chances with the river.

I grab another vine and give it an even stronger tug. This one has to hold, and if it doesn't, I'm a dead man anyway.

There's only space for three running steps before I fling myself over the void. As my feet leave the ground, I keep a firm grip on the vine and try to close myself up in a ball to maximize my momentum. The move works; I'm flying over the precipice in a swift swing. Only, as the other side draws near, I realize I'm not headed for a soft landing. The vine I've picked is barely long enough. I have a split second to make the decision to let go and fling myself the rest of the way. I hover into the air for an instant, limbs flaying, and barely have time to brace myself for the impact. The top half of my body makes it to the soft ferns, while my knees smack against the vertical edge of the cliff.

Ignoring the pain, I scramble for secure hand and toe holds in the vegetation covering the stone. But the root I've placed my weight on snaps and I slide down over the edge before I can find another anchor. Once I'm stable, I crane my neck up at the cliff's edge, fifteen mockingly short inches away. Then, heaven knows why, I stare down. Now I see why they say never to look down. A fresh rush of terror makes my head spin, and I hold on to the roots for dear life.

When I've stopped shivering, I struggle to pull myself up, but can't find a grip strong enough. The rifle slips lower on my back, but I don't try to fasten the strap. I throw my head backward and in a hoarse voice call for help. "Winter!"

"I'm coming," she screams from somewhere above.

Just then the rifle buckle snaps and the weapon falls into the river. I watch its descent in horror. The lost firearm crashes to the bottom and splinters into a million pieces. In an instant, the swarming river has washed away all traces of it.

A speck of rock explodes two inches above my head, sending shards raining over me. I don't have to look back to know that Smith and his men have caught up and are playing target practice with my ass. Another piece of rock shatters below my left foot, and I can only send a small thank-you prayer to my guardian angel they're not equipped with sniper rifles.

"Would you mind hurrying up?" I scream.

"I'm trying," Winter yells. "Grab this." A thick vine falls over the edge.

Spurred on by another bullet just barely missing me, I grab the makeshift rope without testing its resistance and let go of the wall. As I haul myself up, another small explosion splinters the rock where my calf had been a moment ago. With a few forceful pulls, I clear the edge of the cliff and, once on flat ground, I dive under cover.

Winter and I crawl away from the rim into the safety of the jungle just beyond.

"Where's the rifle?" she asks.

"I dropped it."

She curses under her breath. "I could've taken those sorry shots out in a second from here."

"All right, Lara Croft, let's just get our asses out of range; what do you say?"

16

WINTER

Incredibly, this stretch of jungle is even more dense and forlorn than the area we left behind on the other bank of the river. Since the storm clouds rolled away as suddenly as they came, they've been replaced by a thick curtain of steam, rising from the sunbaked rocks and treetops. The humidity in the air must've spiked to 100 per cent. And without the downpour, all kinds of insects have come swarming out of their hives to have a snack— mostly on me. It seems this side of paradise, bugs don't mind being about during the day.

A million bloodsuckers must be infesting this jungle, I swear, and no matter how many I swat away, the flies keep on coming. We didn't grab any chemical repellent spray, and my natural one has no real effect. Mosquitoes, moths, and gnats fly in my face, crawl on my bare skin, and sink their stingers in my exposed flesh. More flesh exposed than normal, thanks to the downhill slide and subsequent struggle through the jungle that have left my clothes in tatters.

Even now, the vegetation tears at them, pointy limbs reach

out and grab at my ruined shirt, which offers little protection against the onslaught. No time to change, though. We need to put as much distance as we can between us and Smith before we can rest.

Ahead of me, Logan isn't fairing any better. His new shirt is hanging off his body in shreds worse than when we came out of the cave, and even if his pants are still in one piece, there are bloodstains on his kneecaps where he hit the cliff. I don't know where he finds the energy to keep hacking at the vines, but he does. We're both pushing beyond our limits.

When by late afternoon the terrain becomes less dense, we call on our last physical reserves. Logan, to swing his machete, and me, simply by putting one foot in front of the other without falling to my knees.

Two hours before dusk, we reach the lower riverbank. Breathless and exhausted, I sink to the ground, not able to move another inch. Logan collapses next to me, sweat pouring down his forehead and soaking his shirt. Hopefully, Smith and his men weren't brave enough to swing across the cliffs like Logan and me. And if they did get across... well, then, we're dead. I physically can't walk another step.

"You think the water is drinkable?" I ask, eyeing the stream.

"Have any purification tablets on you?"

"No."

"Then I wouldn't drink it, not unless you want to spend the next few days squatting down every ten minutes."

"A simple 'no' would've sufficed."

"Oh, you know me." Logan turns to me. "I like to mansplain," he says with self-irony. "But"—his mouth curls up in a wicked grin—"I might let you drink from my canteen if you ask nicely."

"You have water?" I drained my reserves a long while ago.

"I refilled multiple canteens before we left; figured clean water would be a priority."

Nice thinking, Professor.

Mouth parched, I make to grab the bottle from him.

"Not even a please." With a grin, Logan hands me the canteen, cap already off.

I take the bottle from him and gulp down the liquid in lengthy swallows.

"Uh, sorry, but we're back to rationing." Logan pulls the canteen toward himself and, after taking a small sip, screws the cap back on. "We don't know when we'll find fresh water again. And I only have one more bottle after this."

I dry my mouth on the back of my hand and nod in understanding. "Please tell me we can at least wash up in the river water." Dried smears of mud pull at my skin wherever the rainwater didn't reach, making me itchy.

Logan stares at the river. The waters are calm compared to the rapids flowing under the bridge, and there's a natural pool of clear blue-green water that would be perfect to take a bath.

"Tucker would say it isn't safe," Logan muses. "But I want to wash up and change, too. Let's be quick about it, though." He makes a hurry-up gesture. "We need to be done and dry before it gets dark."

Self-consciously, I peel off my tattered clothes. In all the days we've been in the jungle together, this is the first time Logan is my shower buddy. Back at camp, I've mostly gone with Tucker, sometimes Archie. Never Logan.

Okay, I must be this nervous because I'm not wearing a bikini and have to bathe in my underwear. And it's not like I'm clad in a lacy bra and G-string; my black cotton sports bra and panties could pass for a bathing suit. But they aren't. I know it. He knows it.

As I take off my pants, Archie's words from a few days ago ring in my ears louder than gunshots. "It's the sexual tension, honey. Trust me, just get it out of your system and you'll feel better... And hate sex can be amazing."

I pretend not to watch as Logan unbuttons his shredded shirt and lays it over a large rock to dry. His ripped chest and abs, still coated in a thin patina of sweat, glisten enticingly in the late afternoon light.

Before he can look my way and see me half-naked, I wade into the water until I'm neck deep. I undo my tresses and comb my fingers through my hair, rinsing away the last of the mud. I have a clean shirt in my backpack, but no extra pants. So I'd better wash those, too.

"Hey," I call. "Can you throw me my pants? I want to wash them." I eye his, now decorated with twin bloody knee patches. "You should wash yours, too."

Shirtless, Logan throws my pants in the water, where they land a few feet away from me with a loud splash.

I look up at him, ready to give the professor a sarcastic, "Thanks," but when my eyes lock on his, the word gets strangled in my throat. Never taking his gaze off me, Logan undoes his belt, slowly slides it out of its loops, and drops it on the rock at his feet. Then, as he starts unbuttoning his pants, he says, "You might want to take a hold of those before the current carries them away."

Like a slap in the face, his words yank me out of the spell. I glare at his smug smirk and paddle after my pants that are indeed being carried downriver.

By the time I turn again, Logan is cannonballing into the natural pool, his pants flying behind him as he holds them in one hand.

He resurfaces a second later, shaking droplets of water out of his hair.

My mouth goes dry.

Pecs deep in the water, with tiny pearls of the liquid dotting his skin like a million shining crystals, he's the sexiest man I've ever seen.

No. NO. Because he's no man. He's Satan. Better to keep reminding myself; I can't let a few muscles scramble my brain.

But, staring at Logan's glittery skin, that might be easier said than done.

Oh my gosh, I'm experiencing the *Twilight* effect. When Bella sees Edward in direct sunlight for the first time and his skin sparkles. Like Bella with Edward, I can't take my eyes off Logan. He's a demon and has me in his thrall.

Only, having spent so much time alone with him over the past two days, I've learned Dr. Logan Spencer has many more layers than I initially thought. Lately, my hate-Logan wall has been filling with cracks, and right now it feels like it's crumbling down. Yes, he can be gruff and standoffish, but also kind, comforting, brave, sexy as hell...

Here we go again. Somebody, please exorcize me.

"Are you washing those, or what?" Logan asks, a teasing note audible in his voice. As if he's all too aware of the effect his semi-nakedness is having on me. "We should get out soon if we want enough time for our clothes to dry off."

"Yes, I'm washing." I blush and begin to scrub.

Oh, his smug face. The professor thinks he's such a smartass. He wants to play? Let's play.

Once the fabric is cleansed of the mud, I purposely swim in front of Logan and exit the water directly in his line of sight, regaling him with an unobstructed view of my rear side.

Once on the shore, I peek over my shoulder and find him slightly slack-jawed.

"Hey, Doctor?" I call. "Are you washing those, or what?"

He lets out an embarrassed cough. "Yeah, sure. I'll be out in a minute."

I wring as much water as I can out of my pants and sprawl them to dry in the late afternoon sun, then lie on a big flat rock nearby to sunbathe myself.

Logan joins me shortly afterward. For once, I refrain from ogling his body and concentrate on his scraped kneecaps instead.

"Let me dress those," I say, and roll to the side to retrieve the first-aid kit from my backpack.

"Nah, it's nothing," Logan protests.

I ignore him and get to work spraying disinfectant over his bruised skin. "Trust me, you don't want raw skin brushing against your pants."

I cleanse the wounds and dress them with clean gauze, saying, "There you go."

Logan's stare is intense as he says, "Thank you," making me once again hyper-aware of how semi-naked we both are.

"No problem," I say. And, to avoid having to look at him, I lie on my back and close my eyes, enjoying the warmth of the stone beneath me.

In the sweltering heat, my hair and underwear dry off quickly. I grow more comfortable by the minute, until this rock begins to feel like the coziest bed I've ever had. Fatigue catches up with me, and I start to doze off...

When I open my eyes again, the sun is setting and the sky is transitioning from an orange-gold to a dark purple streaked with lavender, and finally a deep violet-blue.

Logan is no longer on the rock with me. I search for him and find him on the riverbank, busy setting up a small tent for the night. A really small tent.

I quickly braid my hair, pull on my pants and the spare shirt from my backpack, collect everything else, and join him near the tent.

"That looks tiny," I say. "Sure it's made to house two?"

"No, it's for one. We'll have to squeeze a little."

I open the flap. "A little? Sleep on top of each other, you mean!"

"Don't be so melodramatic."

"Couldn't you bring a bigger tent?"

"No, sorry. This was the only one still closed, and we didn't exactly have time to pack one of the bigger ones."

"I'm not sleeping in there with you."

"If you want to brave the jungle, be my guest," he says, getting in. "But I'm not staying out here to play meal for the mosquitoes."

As if on cue, the first mosquito bite stings my neck, quelling all my objections. I swat myself, and, with a sigh, follow Logan inside.

* * *

If we sit with our legs held close to our chests, the space is wide enough to allow us to each claim a corner of the tent and not be too much in each other's hair. But if we were to lie down...

One problem at a time.

"What's for dinner?" I ask with an awkward smile.

Logan sorts our food supplies from inside his backpack. "We have a wide assortment of protein bars. Coco Choco... Vanilla Yogurt, Cookie Treat, Fruits & Nuts, and... Choco Peanuts."

"I'll take a Cookie Treat and a Fruits & Nuts."

He tosses them to me and opens one for himself. I can't see the flavor.

"How many do we have left?" I ask.

He does a quick count. "Enough for another day."

"Can we make it back to camp so quickly?"

"We've found the river," Logan says between bites. "So that's good."

"Why?"

"If we cross here where the waters are shallow and follow its course, we won't risk getting lost. It's a small detour; if I remember the map correctly, the river takes a wide bend"—he draws a semicircle in the air with his finger—"that will take us in the wrong direction for a while but then it'll guide us right to our camp."

"Won't that take too long?"

He takes another bite out of his bar and chews pensively. "It's our best option. If we follow the riverbank, we won't have to cut through vines, meaning we should be able to go much faster. No longer than a day."

"If coming this way only takes two days, why didn't we try to reach the lost city from across here in the first place?"

Logan is about to take another bite, but instead, he lowers his bar, dismayed. "Because... did you not notice the gorge we swung across, or the cliff we fell down from? Imagine carrying equipment and supplies that way. We didn't just need to find the city; I wanted to establish an easy route in and out."

I finish my bar and lick my fingers. "Makes sense."

Logan rolls his eyes and I'm honestly tempted to stick out my tongue. But I restrain myself, because I'm the bigger person.

He unscrews the canteen and shakes it. "Water will be a problem soon, though."

Dr. McCheery takes a small sip and hands me the bottle.

I raise it to him in a mock toast.

I'd happily drain the whole thing but force myself to only take an equally small sip and hand it back to Logan.

Meal over, an awkward silence descends. Thankfully, nothing like the dreadful stillness of the treasure chamber. We're surrounded by the sounds of the jungle. Leaves rustling, bats' wings flapping, nocturnal birds hooting... Even the sinister, low growl of distant predators is welcome compared to the unbearable quiet of last night.

"So," I say, unable to bear the stretching silence any longer. "Should we sleep head to toes, or—"

"I'm not sleeping with my head next to your feet."

"Okay, so it's head to head." I flip my hands between us, embarrassed. "Are you coming over here, or am I coming over there?"

Logan pats the floor beside him, in a "come to Papa" gesture.

I scowl but ignore the provocation.

With not enough space to stand or even move that well, we fumble around, trying to shift into position. I'm struggling to lever myself down beside him when my foot slips on the sleek fabric at the bottom of the tent and I land on top of Logan.

Seconds later, my center of gravity is toppled again as I'm rolled onto my back and pressed under a solid wall of hunky archeologist.

Logan's lips slam onto mine, taking me completely by surprise. Before my brain can catch up with what's happening, my body has already taken over, arching against him. My lips have opened and are exploring Logan's mouth. His lips prove as soft and pillowy as they look. I need a taste, so I nip at his lower lip.

Logan is startled and pulls back for a second, but it's enough for me to regain my sanity.

I push him off and scuttle back to my corner. "What are you doing?"

Logan glares at me, confused.

"You kissed me," I accuse.

"And you kissed me back!"

"I did not!"

"You straddled me."

"I lost my balance and fell on top of you."

"And you bit me."

I gasp, outraged. "It was a nibble at most!"

"Whatever." He frantically flips a finger between us. "It wasn't just me."

"It was a reaction, okay? I must be suffering from Stockholm syndrome or something."

"What?" Logan frowns. "I didn't kidnap you."

"But our circumstances are dire enough, it's as if we've been kidnapped together."

"So that's the only reason you kissed me back?"

"It must be. I really don't like you."

"Good. 'Cause I don't like you either."

"Yeah, right," I scoff. "So why did you kiss me, then?"

Logan pouts like a petulant child. "Maybe I'm suffering from Stockholm syndrome, too."

"So we both agree this was a bad idea."

"Really bad idea."

I bite my lower lip. "And we shouldn't do it again."

Logan studies me, looking pained. "That's going to be hard if you keep biting your mouth like that."

I stop torturing my bottom lip and stare at Logan. The atmosphere in this tent is simmering, and not just because we're stranded in a torrid, tropical jungle. Logan and I are kneeling a foot apart, but the air between us feels so dense we could be touching. Tendrils of electricity emanate from our heated bodies and bubble forward to reach the other.

I crack first. "Okay, you can kiss me again," I say, and raise a finger in warning. "But only kissing."

Logan's lips part in a wolfish smile, and, before I can change my mind, he's already cupped the back of my head and pressed those lush pillow lips on mine again.

And, oh gosh, the man kisses me.

Completely.

Thoroughly.

And while he does, his hands roam freely over my body. Nowhere forbidden. But they relentlessly explore every inch of skin that wouldn't land Logan in second or third base territory, making me discover how basically every part of me can be transformed into an erogenous zone. Like the inside of my knee, or the skin on my Achilles tendon, or my collar bone, my neck, arms...

After half an hour of this treatment, my body is burning so much I need to physically remove my clothes.

I push Logan off.

He begins to protest, but stops when I take off my shirt, his eyes darkening.

"What are you doing?" he asks in a low, husky voice.

"I'm hot," I say.

Logan's gaze on my exposed skin is more searing than his hands.

Eyes locked on his, I free my hair from the braids, slowly extricating each strand until soft waves are tumbling over my bare shoulders.

"If you take anything else off, I won't just kiss you," Logan threatens.

Acting bolder than I feel, I unbutton my pants and do my best to shimmy out of them in the confined space of the tent while still trying to look sexy. With one final kick, I toss them to the side and stare down at Logan in a silent challenge.

No turning back now.

17

WINTER

If kissing Logan made my skin burn, making love to him melts all the bones in my body. Under his touch, I lose every sense of self. Exhausted, battered, and running away from trigger-happy lunatics, I've never been more deliriously blissful in my entire life.

Now I get what the fuss about hate sex is.

Only, as Logan's lips brush on mine while our bodies are joined, I'm not sure it's hate that links me to this man at all. His gaze on me is so soul-baring, I can't cope. Unable to deal with my feelings, I close my eyes and let my body take over, losing myself in the moment. Until we both collapse on the tent floor, spent, falling asleep almost immediately in each other's arms.

* * *

The morning after should be awkward, but it isn't. We wake up naked and sweaty, and, as if reading my mind, Logan opens the tent flap and rushes out, yelling, "Last in the water is a loser!"

And who knew the professor, so serious and stern on first

impression, had a playful edge? Last night I got familiar with his sex-god side, but it looks like I'm in for a few more surprises.

I run after him barefooted, laughing as I imagine what Tucker would say if he could witness our total disregard of his jungle safety directives. A few short yards, and I dive in the river head-first, sinking underwater. The liquid streams through my hair and cools my scalp, and nothing has ever felt better—well, except for Logan's hands on my skin last night.

I re-emerge right behind him and splash him. He turns and splashes me back... until his eyes drop to my bare chest and I read the change in them: time to play a whole different game.

We make love in the water, quick and animalistic. Once it's over, Logan gives me another long kiss and carries me out of the river in his arms. He lays me on the rock to dry and walks to the tent, regaling me with a view of his delicious white buns.

When he comes back, he's already wearing his boxer shorts. Logan hands me my clothes and then folds up the one-person tent.

We eat breakfast sitting on the rock in our underwear while our skin dries off. This close to the river, and without the steam from yesterday's storm coating the jungle, there are no insects around to pester us.

Protein bar done with, Logan turns to me. "As much as I'd like to spend all day here with you, we have to get back to camp."

"I know," I say.

We get dressed, collect all our supplies, and once my backpack is nestled once again between my shoulders, I take hold of Logan's hand and interlock our fingers. "Let's go."

* * *

Logan

. . .

We reach the main camp when there's still an hour or so left of daylight. Enough for us to assess the situation while remaining hidden in the bushes at a safe distance.

I squint, but from this far away, I can't tell if the camp has been overrun or not.

"Can you see anything?" I ask.

"No, use this." Winter hands me the miniature telescope again.

I take it and bring the lens to my eye and adjust the focus to scan the circle of tents. In the gap between two of them, I'm able to make out Dr. Boonjan sitting in the dirt on the left side of the camp with a miserable air about himself. Somchai is slouched next to him. Their hands and ankles are tied.

My heart sinks. Smith has wasted no time.

"What's going on?" Winter asks.

"Smith must have control of the camp," I say. "Somchai and Dr. Boonjan are tied up; they're sitting on the ground with their backs against a tree." I observe more closely and notice the length of rope sneaking around their chests. "Bound to the trunk."

"What about Tucker and Archie?"

"I can't see. They must be on the other side of the tree. Let's shift."

Careful not to make any noise, we shuffle sideways, crawling on our elbows and knees. Once we reach our new vantage point, I look through the mini telescope again, clocking in on Archie's ashen features.

Before I can stop myself, an involuntary roar of rage escapes my lips.

Winter pushes my head down toward the ground, and we both lie flat on our bellies.

"Are you crazy?" she hisses. "You want to get us caught? What did you see?"

"It's Archie," I say. "I have to go."

I try to push up again, but she pulls me back to the ground, saying, "Calm down."

"Check for yourself"—I hand her the telescope—"and then tell me again to calm down."

Winter takes the black tube from me and spies the camp through the high grass covering the terrain. I know when she has Archie in her focus, because she gasps loudly.

"Those bastards," Winter whispers angrily, without removing her eye from the lens. "They've made him sit on his wounds." She pauses, takes another look, and gasps even louder. "There's blood on the ground; the stitches must have burst open. He has to be in a lot of pain."

I take the telescope back from her and examine my best friend's face. "It's not just the pain. He's not well. An infection, most likely. Smith must've gotten here last night. If Archie has been sitting in the dirt with open wounds for twenty-four hours, he must already be feverish. We have to do something."

"Agreed," Winter says, and preventively grabs my arm to ground me. "But rushing in there won't solve a thing."

"It's Archie." I struggle to get free. "I have to go."

"Logan." The tenderness in her voice makes me pause. "Say you attack now, and even manage to cut them free. Then what?" She pauses. "Archie will need to be carried at this point. Tucker looks more like a teddy bear than someone who'd be helpful in a fight." No matter how fit he is, I add in my head. To go against Smith, one needs to be mean, and Tucker doesn't have an ounce of mean in him. "And the only thing Dr. Boonjan has fought in his life," she continues, "is probably an unruly book page. So unless Somchai has some hidden martial arts skills, you'd be in there alone fighting three highly trained ex-Special Forces armed to the teeth with no weapons of your own. You'd only get yourself caught and tied to the tree with the others. Then Archie would really stand no chance."

Winter's right. I hate that she's right. And not because she has outsmarted me once again; because it means I'm powerless to help my best friend when he needs me the most.

"So what do you propose?" I ask.

"We wait."

"For what?"

"It's almost dark. If the soldiers haven't left by now, they must be planning to leave at first light tomorrow."

"I'm not sure Archie has that much time."

"Listen to me, Logan, we're his only hope and we only get one shot at this, so we have to get it right on the first try."

"You have a plan?"

Winter winks at me. "I do."

I shake my head. I swear, this woman never ceases to amaze me.

* * *

While we wait for the cover of night, we retreat further away from the camp to drink the last of our last water, split the remaining protein bar, and rest. We hide our backpacks in a thick bush and stand by until the jungle is coated in darkness.

Then, hiding in the shadows, we crawl back toward the assembly of tents. The camp lights provide just enough illumination for us to check on the state of things through the telescope.

"The prisoners are still in the same spot," I say. "You think they're feeding them? Giving them water?"

"I don't know," Winter replies. "But let's focus on our mission right now. You have eyes on Smith?"

"Yeah, he's with his minions having dinner under the tarp."

The three of them are sitting around the table with a lantern placed in its center, eating and talking. Voices carry out to us, but not loud enough for us to pick up what they're saying. The bastards are laughing, most likely discussing all the ways they're going to spend their loot.

"What of the rifles?" Winter asks.

I squint against the darkness. At their feet, I catch a glint of moonlight reflected on black metal: the armory and ammunition box.

"They're guarding them closely."

"Good," Winter says. "Just as we imagined. Smith knows we're out here, weaponless. He must've figured that if we tried something, we'd go for the artillery first. What about the phones and laptop?"

As the moon rises higher in the sky, the scene before us becomes clearer still. "Smith has my phone case next to him. The laptop, too," I say. "He's literally keeping it under his arm."

"What about Tucker's phone?"

I search and search, but... "I can't see it anywhere."

"Could it still be in his tent?" Winter asks hopefully. "Did Smith know Tucker had a second satellite phone?"

"Let's hope he didn't," I say grimly.

We crawl a few yards back, keeping out of sight.

Waiting.

Again.

I hate waiting.

Winter shuffles closer to me, and her lips find mine in the

darkness. And for a second nothing else exists anymore. Just me and this woman. This fierce, brave, insufferable person that has stolen much more from me than Smith and his puppets ever could. She has taken my heart, and now it's hers to do with as she pleases.

We find comfort in each other. Saying with tender kisses and caresses what's too hard to put into words. Trying to cure the other of the fear we're both feeling for Archie. For ourselves.

The sudden silence shakes us to attention.

"Have they gone to sleep?" Winter asks.

"Let's go check."

As stealthily as we can, we slither back to our vantage point. With the camp's lights out, the half-moon provides just enough light for us to see that the camp is still. All is quiet.

"Looks like they've retired for the night," I say.

"They didn't leave anyone to guard the camp?"

My eyes go at once to where I spotted the armory box last. Poking out from inside the tent next to it, there's a boot. And, judging from the angle the foot is at, it must belong to someone sitting on a chair.

"Someone is guarding the weapons and coms," I say. "Just as you predicted. But I don't know who it is; I can't see their face."

I can only hope it's not Smith, I add silently in my head. We stand a better chance if one of his brainless pals is the only person awake out there.

"Okay," Winter says. "Let's wait another half an hour just to be on the safe side, and then we go in as planned."

I nod, even though I have no intention of sticking to the plan.

18

LOGAN

"It's time," Winter says a while later.

I squeeze her hand to let her know I've heard her.

We start to circle back toward the camp, Winter in front of me. But I stop at once. With the moon completely risen, her head of white-blonde hair stands out in the darkness like a beacon.

"Wait," I call-whisper.

"What?"

"Your hair, it's too light, it's unmissable. I could spot it from a mile away."

"Logan, I'm not staying behind," she threatens.

"I wasn't suggesting you did," I say. "Come here," I add, and quickly pull one of my dark shirts out of my backpack.

When she reaches me, I wrap her hair under the fabric, securing the shirt around her head with two tight knots.

She smiles at me throughout the whole process, the hint of flirtation clear on her face—which, by the way, shines just as bright as the hair. Even after two weeks in the tropical sun, her skin is still pearly white and too reflective even in the faint moonlight.

Without giving her any warning, I sink my hands in the moist dirt and smear a generous amount across her cheeks.

Winter sputters in protest. "What are you doing?"

"Covering your face," I say, adding a smudge to her forehead. "Your skin is too light as well."

"Really?" She scowls. "You seem to be enjoying yourself an awful lot, Dr. Spencer."

And, if in the beginning her calling me Dr. Spencer used to annoy me... now the title has a whole different effect.

Not the time.

"It's for your protection," I reply, dead serious.

"Well, in that case." She sinks her hands into the muddy ground and returns the favor, saying, "If you're into dirty foreplay."

And even though the circumstances are so dire, she manages to crack a smile out of me.

Once the camouflage is complete, we resume the journey toward Tucker's tent. My muscles scream in protest from all the crouching and crawling, and my body hurts everywhere. The amazing woman next to me must be in the same state of pain and exhaustion, but not a single complaint escapes her lips. And I can't help it; my chest swells with pride, as if her endurance was my merit somehow.

When we reach the other side of the camp, Winter starts forward toward Tucker's tent, but I pull her back.

She looks at me questioningly.

"You go get the phone," I whisper. "There's something else I have to do."

"What?" she hisses. "Logan, no! We have a plan; you stick to the plan."

"I can't. I can't leave Archie like that. I have to find him an antibiotic and some water."

A ray of moonlight hits Winter's face, and I can see the fear in her features while her brain cogs are furiously at work.

"You get the phone," she says after a while. "I'll find the medicine and water for Archie."

"What? No!" I protest. "It's too dangerous."

"I've never been inside Tucker's tent," Winter protests. "I have no idea where he keeps the phone and stand no chance of finding it in the dark. And even if I did, I don't know how it works. The antibiotics are in the supply tent, I know the layout, I can get to them more easily," she says with finality. "We meet again where we left the backpacks."

And before I can protest further, she dashes in the opposite direction. I suppress a curse that my plan not to stick to the plan has majorly backfired on me and put her in more danger.

I sigh. Nothing I can do about it now; I have to focus on the task ahead.

I approach Tucker's tent from the back, slither Smith's knife out of its sheath, and cut a vertical opening in the tent's fabric. Before going in, I check the path is clear by spying between the gap. The front of Tucker's tent is zipped down, and there's no one inside. Perfect. No one will be able to spot me from the camp.

I slip in and squat on the floor, suddenly disoriented. Without the moonlight filtering in from outside, I'm in complete darkness. Blind, I carefully place the knife back in its sheath so I don't accidentally stab myself. Then I search the surrounding space with my hands. My fingers finally clasp Tucker's cot. I grab it and, even if it doesn't make much of a difference, given the poor light, I close my eyes, trying to remember the layout of my friend's tent. The window flap should be somewhere above the bed.

I climb on the cot, my heart jumping in my throat when the metal springs squeak. I pause, breathing heavily, while my pulse races into a frenzy and my ears strain for any sign the noise has been heard and that I've been discovered. But the night mercifully stays quiet. My thoughts go out to Winter. What is she doing? Has she reached the supply tent? If they catch her... I have to crush the panic rising in my chest. Seeing her trapped once has been enough for a lifetime. Not an experience I care to repeat.

Don't be silly, Logan, that woman is ten times tougher than any men around here. No way a night incursion is what takes her out.

Right.

She's probably already waiting at the rendezvous point, wondering what's taking me so damn long.

Searching the tent's wall with my fingertips, I finally come into contact with the flap. I roll it up and tie it with the small string attached in its center. The window isn't big, but it lets enough moonlight into the tent for me to make out shapes. I give my eyes a few more seconds to adjust, and then begin my exploration.

I'm sure the soldiers searched all the tents, so if they didn't find the phone, it means Tucker must've stashed it somewhere out of sight. But where?

I climb off the bed and search the ground underneath. Nothing here.

Next, I move in a clockwise circle around the tent, searching every box, bag, and crevice I can find.

Nothing.

The blasted phone is nowhere to be found.

I sink back on my haunches, racking my brain. Where could my friend have put it?

My eyes drift back to his backpack. I've already patted it, and it was only soft fabric inside. Clothes. Nothing more.

But maybe the army guys performed the same superficial search and came to the same conclusion.

I kneel in front of the rucksack and resolve to try every last pocket. When I've removed a dozen folded T-shirts, my hands finally bump against something solid. My fingers fasten around a plastic handle, and I pull out the phone case, touching it to my lips. I quickly throw all the discarded clothes back in the sack and restore it to the spot where I found it.

I consider climbing on the bed once again to close the window flap, but I doubt even Smith would notice such a tiny detail. And, anyway, if they come looking, the slash in the back wall will be enough to give away the nightly incursion.

Decision made, I slip out of the tent the way I came in and scamper far away. Giving the camp a wide berth, I retrace my steps to the spot where Winter and I left our meager supplies.

She isn't there.

My heart falls.

My first instinct is to run back and go look for her, but the ghost of her voice prevents me. "You stick to the plan."

Right. Even if, worst-case scenario, they caught Winter, the best I can do right now is call for reinforcements. That's the first priority. At least that way, when I go look for her and probably get myself captured in the attempt, there will be help on the way.

I take the phone out of the case and squat low behind a bush to screen the inbuilt light from sight—in the surrounding darkness, it'd have the same effect as an emergency flare and give away my position, especially if Winter has been found out and Smith is looking for me. On the retro-illuminated green screen, I scroll for preloaded numbers and dial the emergency number of the American embassy in Bangkok.

They pick up on the first ring.

"Hello, this is a distress call from Dr. Logan Spencer..."

* * *

Winter

Before Logan can start an argument and get both of us caught, I crawl away from him, ending the discussion. The ground is hard under my hands and knees, dotted with small, pointy rocks that attack the flesh of my bare palms and tear at the fabric of my pants each time I move. But I've become accustomed to the pain; I've lost count of the cuts and bruises on my skin. I swear, if I get out of this alive, I'm going to spend the next month in a Thai spa immersed in a coconut milk and jasmine oil bath, and I'm coming out only to be massaged.

Mmm. The thought of moisturizing lotion, of a hot bath, almost makes me cry with longing. Why couldn't I be one of those photographers who are content doing weddings and baby photoshoots? No, I had to seek adventure...

Aha!

I've had enough adventure for a lifetime.

A loud snore makes me stop in my tracks and jerks me back to the here and now of my mission. In the semi-darkness, it's hard to get properly oriented, but I've passed two tents since Tucker's—Logan's and Archie's—which means I'm at the main gathering tent. Right behind where the sentry is stationed. Did they fall asleep?

I strain my ears and, there, barely audible amidst the night noises of the rainforest, is the faint breathing of someone fast asleep. And, yep, another soft snoring sound.

So it's definitely not Smith on guard; he'd never sleep on the job. Not with his enemies still out there. But the other two are cockier—don't see us as a real threat, I suppose. And thank goodness for that; we need a bit of luck for our plan to work. If we get caught, Archie is dead. Maybe we're all dead. Who knows what Smith and his minions intend to do with the prisoners.

Still moving carefully—soldiers are renowned for being light sleepers—I proceed to the next tent, my destination.

There, I stop, cursing under my breath. I don't have a knife to cut my way in from the back as Logan must've done in Tucker's tent by now. That's why there was a plan, and why people should stick to said plan: so I don't find myself in need of a knife I didn't bring as I try to break into a tent no one was supposed to touch.

Nothing good comes out of improvising.

What do I do now?

Well, no other way in than from the front. I take a deep breath and thank my fairy godmother that Logan camouflaged my face and hair, and that Smith didn't take the first watch. Thank you, thank you, thank you, Fairy Godmother. I mean, some girls need a princess gown and a carriage to bring them to the ball. But not me; I'm more the need-an-asleep-soldier-and-camouflaged-face kind of gal.

Slower than before, I crawl forward, keeping my left side close to the wall of the supply tent—the one furthest away from the sleeping sentry. When I reach the end, I peek just my head out of cover and try to assess the situation.

I can make out a dark shape slumped on a chair in the next tent, one booted foot on the ground and the other resting on the armory box. The face is hidden in the shadows, but I'm surer than ever it must be Carter or Montgomery. In the two weeks we've been here, I've never seen Smith not standing to attention. He probably even sleeps rigid as a pole.

I examine the supply tent beside me and sigh in relief when the entry flap flutters in the night breeze. It's open! If I had to pull the zipper all the way up, I would've died of a heart attack; but with it already unlatched, I can just slither in. I take a few extra seconds to steady my pulse and then scramble forward in a desperate dash.

Inside the tent, I crouch in the middle and pause again, giving my eyes time to adjust to the deeper darkness and straining my ears for any alarm sound. None comes. I haven't been spotted.

Okay, the medical case was in the far-right corner of the tent last time I used it. I head that way. I search, using my hands more than my eyes; the only light filters in from the moving entrance flap, and it's not nearly enough to see by properly.

I grab a case and open it, brushing my fingers over the contents.

No, it's a toolbox.

I move on to the next case.

Radio equipment.

Could we use radios to call for help? Mmm, I don't know how to operate them, and even if Logan does, in all likelihood they're short-range. I discard the box and move to the next case, and...

Bingo! The medkit.

My triumph is short-lived. There are dozens of pill bottles inside, and I have no way of telling the paracetamol from the antibiotics from the Imodium. So I take all the bottles and stuff my pockets full.

Now, water.

It takes me forever to find a half-full canteen. When I do, I clutch the bottle to my chest, but I can't crawl with it in my hands, so I shove it down the front of my shirt, securing the neck under my bra strap.

I'm already lifting the flap to retrace my steps when a voice cuts through the night.

"Dude." There's a dull sound, like that of one boot kicking another. "Are you sleeping?"

With a snort, the sentry awakens.

Heart beating to a frenzy in my throat, I crab-walk backward toward the center of the tent. The rattle of the pills in my pockets pounds in my ears, seeming louder than cannon shots. I sit to give my legs a rest. Still like a stone and bathed in almost utter darkness, I dread even the sound of my breathing will be too loud.

"You're lucky it was me, dude," the same voice says. "Smith would've taken your scalp."

"Relax, my man. No one's here. And I had my boots on the weapons all along, didn't I? No one is going to sneak past me."

If the situation wasn't so tragic, I'd evil-laugh.

"All right, man," the guy who was sleeping continues. "Your gig now. Run it as you like."

There's a scraping noise, and then the shuffling of steps until everything goes quiet again. A new sentry, and I have a feeling this one won't conveniently fall asleep for me.

What now?

I can't risk going out the way I snuck in. Not with a freshly awakened, alert soldier out there. The chances he'd spot me leaving the tent are too high. I have to find something to cut my way out from the back. Good thing I'm in a supply tent; there must be a tool in here I can use.

A thousand times more careful not to make a sound than before, I grope for the toolbox. When I find it, I unhinge the plastic locks, their soft clicks echoing too loudly in my ears, and feel my way through the various tools. I sigh in relief when my fingers slide over a cutter.

Blade in hand, I find a spot of wall clear of supplies and try to steady my hand as I slice a vertical opening in the sturdy fabric. The cutter must be new, because it slices downward as if I were cutting through butter.

Outside, I close the cutter and pocket it. Okay, now the hard part. I move away from the camp until I find a small clearing where a ray of moonlight is filtering through the trees above. The faint light is enough for me to read the pill labels and identify the antibiotics and the paracetamol. Archie was shivering like he was burning up, so paracetamol should help to take his temperature down. And even if he's not feverish, I bet he could use a little help managing the pain.

I hide the rest of the pill bottles in a patch of grass; I can't risk getting confused when I have to give them to Archie. Summoning the last dregs of energy and courage I have left, I keep going toward the prisoners' corner. I'm not far now.

Once there, I stop again, considering. My friends are all asleep, slumped as best as they can against the tree. A pang of worry pulls at my chest as I notice Archie's head hanging lower than all the others.

This is the tricky part.

How do I get to them without being spotted by the sentry?

The prisoners aren't directly in his line of view, but the soldier must have at least a partial visual on them—and judging from the way they are oriented, on Archie in particular.

Damn!

What do I do?

Tucker is sitting next to Archie, and he should be shielded enough from the soldier's position. My best bet is to hand the pills to Tucker and have him give them to Archie. Assuming he's able to do it tied up like that. But first I need to wake him without him making a sound, and thus giving our game away.

I crawl right in front of him and place my palm squarely on his mouth.

Tucker's eyes fly wide open, but my hand prevents him from crying out.

"Shhh," I whisper. "It's me, Winter."

With my face covered in dirt, I must be unrecognizable and possibly frightening. But Tucker is quicker than I would've been in recovering from the shock and gives me a curt nod. So I let my hand drop from his mouth and press a finger to my lips.

Tucker stares at me interrogatively, and I don't need him to actually ask what's going on for me to understand the unspoken question.

"We don't have much time," I explain. "Logan is looking for your satellite phone to call for help. I brought antibiotics and paracetamol for Archie, and some water. How long have you been stuck here?"

"Since yesterday morning," Tucker whispers back, his voice hoarse.

"How is he?"

"Not good. It's been hours since I felt him move, and he's burning up."

"Okay, give these to him." I press the antibiotic pills into his hand. "But careful the guard doesn't spot you."

Tucker lifts his tied-up hands to Archie's mouth and forces the pills in, while I keep to the side and out of sight of the sentry. A low moan escapes our friend's lips.

"Make him swallow them," I hiss.

"I can't lift his head." Tucker shows me his bound wrists as an explanation. "You'll have to give him the water."

Hands shaking with fear of getting caught, I retrieve the

canteen from the folds of my shirt, unscrew the top and, keeping as much to the side as I can—I'm basically straddling poor Tucker—I gently lift Archie's head. When his chin is tilted up at the right angle, I press the bottle to his lips. He's still unconscious, but some primordial survival instinct must prompt him to drink. Like a baby sucking at the bottle, in a few deep gulps he finishes the water. As soon as I let go, Archie's chin slumps back to his chest with a slight loll. But at least he's taken the pills.

Crouching back on the ground, I give Tucker the remaining antibiotics and paracetamol.

"I don't have any more water. Sorry."

Tucker nods.

"I have to go now. But hold tight." I squeeze his knee in an encouraging gesture. "Reinforcements will come soon."

We exchange another, more meaning-loaded nod, and I scamper away.

I find Logan waiting in our spot, evidently going mad with worry.

"What took you so long?" he demands, the moment I step out of the darkness.

"Sorry, I had a couple of snafus—"

"Shut up," he interrupts, pulling me into a bone-crushing hug that lets me know how much he'd been worried.

Still hugging, we sink to the ground and lie down to sleep, not bothering to even lay a blanket before sheer exhaustion makes both of us pass out in each other's arms.

19

LOGAN

The pain in my back wakes me up the next morning even before the first sunrays filter through the jungle's dense canopy. But dawn is close, and the day promises to be another scorcher in this blasted furnace of a jungle.

As I stir, my body hurts even more than yesterday, if that's possible. Lactic acid is attacking my every joint, and every muscle in my limbs is screaming in protest. Sleeping on the humid ground hasn't helped either, I bet.

I shake Winter awake, and from the way she winces in pain before she even opens her eyes, I can tell she's not faring much better.

We don't have any food or water left, and the stomach cramps just add to our general state of misery. But at least we're free, and we have each other.

Winter smiles at me. Last night we fell asleep before we even had time to discuss our respective missions. I assume she succeeded, or she would have said something, but I still want to hear it from her lips.

"Did you manage to get to Archie?"

"Yeah, and I gave Tucker some extra pills, too. Did you call for help?"

"Yep, Smith's coup should be over soon. The good guys are on the way."

"So, what now? We just wait?"

"I guess. And we should keep an eye on the camp, although I'm not sure how we can stop Smith if he decides to hurt our friends."

"I'm sure we can think of something. Did they say how long before the police get here?"

"No. I talked with a clerk at the embassy, but the phone died halfway through the conversation. I managed to give them our exact position before the line got cut off, and also stressed the direness of the situation. They should arrive soon. But I want to check on Archie anyway, make sure the drugs worked."

Winter nods. "Let's go."

When we reach our previous vantage point, we lay flat on our bellies and monitor the clearing through Winter's telescope. The camp is already stirring with activity. Smith & Co. are loading the mule, and it looks like they'll be ready to take off at any minute.

I train the magnifying glass on Archie's face next, and sigh with relief. Some color has returned to his cheeks, and he's sitting up much straighter than yesterday. His head isn't lolling lifelessly to the side anymore, and his eyes are open and attentive. Still, the grimace of pain that pulls at my best friend's mouth is unmistakable.

"What do you see?" Winter asks.

"Archie is much better; here"—I push the telescope into her hands—"see for yourself."

As she looks, I kiss her temple. "Thank you; it's all because of you."

Nothing significant happens for about half an hour, while the soldiers are busy with their preparations. But once they're done, Carter asks Smith the question I've been dreading all along, "What about the prisoners, sir?"

Smith, eyes dark and cold as those of a falcon, turns toward our friends and colleagues and frowns.

A sense of foreboding takes residence in my gut. I don't like that scowl. I don't like it one bit.

Smith's eyebrows draw closer together, and he walks over to the prisoners and squats right in front of Archie.

"Well, Mr. Hill, if you don't look rosy as a peach this fine morning." He roughly pulls Archie's hair to lift his head and presses the back of his other hand to my friend's forehead. "No fever, either. Carter! Montgomery!"

Like obedient dogs, his minions immediately respond to the summons.

"Sir."

"Sir."

"It seems we have a bit of a miracle on our hands..."

"Sir?" Carter repeats.

"Our esteemed guest, Mr. Hill, has prodigiously recovered from his fever. Now, I'm not much of a spiritual man myself... so I suspect we might've had a pair of unwanted visitors last night. Two little critters sneaking in the dark. Carter, Montgomery, did you notice anything unusual during your guards?"

"No, sir," Montgomery says at once.

"Carter?"

Carter shuffles on his feet, uncomfortable, but Smith doesn't even have to talk to convince him to speak. The colonel's mean stare is enough of a threat. "Sir, I found Montgomery asleep at his post when I relieved him of his duty at zero three hundred hours last night, sir."

Montgomery looks affronted for a second at being ratted out like that, but he doesn't have much time to show his indignation before Smith makes his head snap sideways with a backhanded blow. "You idiot! Search all the tents. I want to know where they went and what they took."

Next to me, Winter tenses. "What do we do now?"

"Nothing. Even if they figure out what we took, they don't know where we are."

"What if they come searching for us?"

"I doubt Smith will want to lose precious time coming after us."

"Sir!"

A shout makes us turn our eyes back to the camp. We watch as Smith walks toward the supply tent, while Montgomery relates his findings. "There's a tear in the back of the tent, sir; the supplies are in disarray and most of the medicines are gone."

"So, Mr. Hill's miraculous recovery is explained. Carter! You find anything?"

"Yes, sir." The other soldier joins them. "I found a similar tear in Wallace's tent."

"Mmm." Smith ponders this for a moment, then walks back to the prisoners. "It's obvious why they went after the medicines in the supply tent, but..." Smith squats in front of Tucker. "Hey, Jonas Brother, what were they looking for in your tent?"

"I don't know," Tucker says.

"Really?" Menacing as a cobra, Smith rises to his feet, unsheathes his handgun from his belt, and points it at Tucker's head. "I'd love to interrogate you the old-fashioned way, buddy, but unfortunately there ain't time for that. So either you tell me what's going on, or"—he lowers the gun—"I bust your kneecaps. The right first, then the left."

Tucker, talk, I pray silently. No point in playing the hero.

A cold rage fills me at how powerless we are against these brutes.

"Come on," Smith threatens. "Don't make me count to ten."

"My gun, okay?" Tucker snaps. "I had a gun hidden in my backpack. Logan knew about it."

Winter gasps next to me. "Why is Tucker telling them we have a gun?"

"He's being smart," I say. "He doesn't want them to realize we called for help."

"But why?"

"Because if Smith knows about the reinforcements, he might change his plan—take a different path, maybe bring along some of the prisoners as hostages... Right now, the only threat he knows about is us. And I think he considers us more of an annoyance than anything."

"Yeah, but now they think we have a gun," Winter says. "Smith won't stand for that. He'll come after us just the same."

"He still has to find us first."

Smith takes a few steps back, still clutching his Beretta in one meaty hand.

"Dr. Spencer, Miss Knowles!" he shouts. "How very impolite of you not to stay for breakfast. Now I feel like you just used me for a night's fun and left me to hang the next morning." He approaches the prisoners again and points the gun at Archie's head. "I suggest you don't try anything funny with that gun you stole, or I'll blow Mr. Hill's head right off. A pity, really, after all the effort you've put into saving his life. And even if you shoot me first"—he makes a jerking motion with his chin at Carter—"Carter here will take care of Mr. Hill for me."

The sergeant takes out his own gun and points it at Archie, while Smith keeps shouting threats. "I'm sure none of us would want that, now, would we?"

Winter and I both keep dead still on the ridge, looking aghast at the scene below us, unsure what to do.

"No need to act like children," Smith continues. "Do I really have to count to ten?"

We still don't move.

"All right. You have until ten. One... Two..."

I turn to Winter. "I have to go."

"Three..."

"What? No! Are you crazy?"

"Four..."

"It makes no difference if they have me, too," I say. "But you stay hidden right here."

"Five..."

"If you're going, I'm going," Winter protests.

"Six..."

"No, you're not."

"Seven..."

"Logan, please."

"Eight. I'm running out of patience. Nine..."

I stand up, shouting, "I'm coming!"

All the soldiers' heads turn toward our hiding place, and Montgomery points his gun at my chest.

"Good boy," Smith says, not lowering the gun pointed at Archie. Neither does Carter. "Now come down very slowly, hands above your head, and don't try anything funny. You, too, Miss Knowles. We all know you're the real shooter of the group."

Before I can tell Winter to stay hidden, she stands up, shrugging at me in a what-was-I-supposed-to-do? way.

We draw courage from each other as, hands raised above our heads, we walk down the hill to join the others.

"Search them," Smith orders as we step into the camp. "I want that gun."

Carter pats me down while Montgomery drags his hands all over Winter's body. I've never felt anything more violent than the rage rising in my chest at seeing the filthy soldier's hands on her.

"Sir," Carter says. "He's clean."

"Yeah," Montgomery echoes. "Her, too."

"So, where's the gun?" Smith asks.

"I dropped it," Winter says. "When you started shouting. You startled me, and it slid down the hill before I could grab it."

"Oh, really?" Smith looks unconvinced. He's no fool; he knows something's off. "Carter, go check if you can find a gun where Miss Knowles has indicated."

With a sinking heart, I watch Carter trek up the hill.

What happens when he gets there and finds nothing? They'll start asking questions, that's what, and if they threaten Winter I'll tell them everything.

"Sir!" Carter shouts after a few minutes. "There's nothing here."

"Why am I not surprised?" Smith says. "So, where's the gun?"

Winter stares at me, eyes wide. We've run out of excuses. I'm sure Smith can read the lies on our scared expressions.

"Okay, Dr. Spencer, I tried to be reasonable, but I really don't have time to play games," Smith says. He steps behind Winter, wraps one arm around her waist, and points his gun directly at her temple.

20

WINTER

The metal is cold against my skin.

It's a sharp contrast to Smith's warm, rancid breath, which grazes past my ear when he speaks next. "You know the drill, Dr. Spencer. Tell me where the gun is, or..." He joggles the Beretta against my temple. "One..."

I always imagined having a gun pointed at my head would be more terrifying. Well, not that I've ever really pictured myself being taken hostage before today. I never thought I'd find myself in such a predicament. But now that I'm standing here, literally looking down the barrel of life and death, the experience is surreal. As if it were happening to someone else. Honestly, I half expect a camera crew to jump out of the bushes and scream, "You've been Punk'd!" any time now.

The psychology behind such a reaction is pretty straightforward: our bodies respond to life-threatening situations by creating a rush of adrenaline, supplying us with courage we don't normally have. Providing a willingness to fight when exhaustion should've taken it away.

So here I stand, brave in the face of death. If I have to kick the bucket today, I'll go with my head held high, staring into the eyes of the man I love. Not the worst way to die, I suppose.

"Two..."

But as I stare at Logan, I don't see the same resolution in his hazel eyes. He's too afraid for me. He's going to cave and tell Smith all about the satellite phone and help being on the way. And then the colonel will pack us all off before the Thai police can get here.

But I don't blame Logan. I'd do the same if it were him with a gun pointed at his head.

"Thr—"

The bushes around the camp explode into life. In a blur, heavily camouflaged soldiers emerge from the jungle, and before our captors have time to realize what's happening, the newcomers overpower Carter and Montgomery. Guns pried from their hands, they're made to lie flat on their bellies, faces smashed into the dirt, while our saviors bind their wrists behind their backs with zip ties.

But there's still the small matter of Smith holding a gun to my head. The colonel and I both realize what's happening at the same time; I can tell by his grip tightening around my waist.

"Let the girl go," one of the armed newcomers orders, pointing his rifle at us—at Smith—along with three other members of his commando unit. That makes it a total of one gun and four assault rifles pointed at me.

Smith snickers. "That would be really stupid on my part, wouldn't it? You can't shoot me while I'm—"

Something hisses in the air below my ear and passes beside my neck. Smith goes limp without warning, his body slumping down behind mine. As he hits the ground, Smith's hand falls open and the Beretta scatters in the dirt.

I hear screaming, and it takes me a while to understand it's me. Smith's dead! All the fear, tension, and exhaustion of the past few days erupts out of me in strangled screams.

"Miss, miss." A soldier is holding my shoulders and shaking me.

"You killed him!" I shout, in shock, feeling the side of my face for blood that isn't there.

"Miss, he's just taking a nap." The soldier turns me, forcing me to stare down at Smith. And, indeed, the colonel's features are relaxed, his mouth slightly turned up at the corners in a serene, contented smile. "We used a powerful sedative dart, not a bullet."

I grip the soldier's arm. "Smith's alive?"

"Yes, ma'am. He's probably having a better time than we are." The soldier gently squeezes my shoulders and lets me go. "But I promise the music will change when he wakes up."

"And how come you're going around with a tranquilizer gun? Is that standard equipment for the army?"

"No." The soldier smiles. "We were on a search and rescue for an American tiger that got lost in the jungle—"

"What's an American tiger doing so far from home?"

"She's a rare species, and was here for reproductive reasons when she escaped..."

"Oh," I say. "And are you still going to retrieve her?"

"That's our next stop, miss, once we're done dealing with these fine gentlemen."

The soldier unceremoniously flips the colonel's unconscious body in the dirt, not bothering to be gentle, and binds his hands behind his back.

The shock is passing now, and I turn to meet Logan's eyes. He opens his arms, and I fly into them, collapsing in a fit of sobs against his chest. I don't even know why I'm crying, or if they're happy or sad tears.

Logan shushes me, while he holds me tight and gently caresses my back in a soothing motion. "It's over now."

"Err..." Someone clears his throat next to us, and we pull apart. "Sorry to interrupt." It's a different soldier, still wearing his netting-covered helmet. "Are you Dr. Logan Spencer?"

"Yes," Logan says.

"I'm Colonel Sanchez, responsible for the operation."

Logan smiles brightly. "Never been more pleased to meet someone, Colonel."

The colonel acknowledges Logan's implicit thanks with a curt nod. "I just need to confirm all the armed parties have been apprehended. There were only three, correct?"

"Correct."

"And you said you had a gravely injured man in your midst?"

With a sinking feeling of guilt, we both turn to the prisoners' encampment. I'd forgotten all about them in the drama of the moment. Archie is being helped to his feet by Tucker and another soldier; it's clear he still isn't strong enough to stand on his own. Next to them, Dr. Boonjan and Somchai are drinking water in long, thirsty gulps.

"Yes," Logan says. "The blond man. He's in need of immediate medical attention."

We watch as Tucker sways slightly under Archie's weight. A second soldier takes his place, and both Tucker and Archie are given water.

"The rest of us should be fine," Logan says. "Except for mild dehydration."

The colonel nods. "Our medic will have a look at your colleague, and we have a helicopter on standby. I'm calling it now. We're flying your friend to Bangkok."

When the helicopter arrives, there isn't a stretch of flat

ground large enough for it to land, so they hover as close to the ground as they can and pass down a stretcher.

The two soldiers holding Archie upright act as human crutches as he limps toward the gurney.

"On my belly, please," Archie pleads.

The soldiers help him turn and lower him down, securing him to the cot.

Logan and I kneel next to Archie's head, the wind and noise of the rotating blades roaring above us. Logan takes his hand and shouts, "I'm going to see you soon!"

"Yeah, not so easy to get rid of me," Archie jokes feebly. His eyes flick to me. "I owe you my ass, Snowflake—twice over!"

Fresh tears threaten to spill from my eyes, and I bend down to stamp a soft kiss on his left temple.

"Please stand back," a medic in uniform requests. "We have to hoist him up now."

We take a step back and crane our necks up, waving as Archie is hauled onto the helicopter. The men on board pull him in, and then the powerful machine rises higher in the sky and quickly disappears from view.

"Dr. Spencer," Colonel Sanchez calls. "The embassy has arranged for a military convoy to escort you from the nearest village to Trat's airport. Horses should arrive soon to transport you back to the village. I assume you'll all want to leave today, yes?"

"What about the site?" Logan asks, the archeologist in him prevailing over the exhausted man.

"The Thai police are on their way to secure the perimeter and make sure no pillaging takes place."

Even after the colonel's reassuring words, the struggle is easy to read on Logan's face. Part of him wants to stay and ensure his discovery is not tampered with, but the rest of him is dying to be at Archie's bedside.

Dr. Boonjan drops a heavy hand on Logan's shoulder. "Go look after your friend," he says. "I can stay behind and make sure everything is handled properly. I watched them load the treasure onto that poor mule—I'll make sure that's properly cataloged as well."

"Are you sure?" Logan asks. "You don't want to go back, take a shower, sleep in a real bed?"

Dr. Boonjan's lips part in a rare grin. "I've slept in worse places, and I've never taken a more scenic bath than by the river here. You, on the other hand, look like you could use that shower."

Logan, his face and body still covered in mud, laughs. "I suppose we could."

"Take care of Archibald," Dr. Boonjan says. "I'll handle things here until you can come back."

Logan nods at him, and then turns to Colonel Sanchez. "Colonel, we're ready to leave whenever you are."

21

WINTER

Two days later, in Bangkok, I wiggle my toes under the foam of the bubble bath I'm taking in the hotel's tub. We checked in last night, after first visiting Archie at the hospital. His prognosis is good. Our sweet Viking will be back on his feet in no time.

"If you stay in that tub any longer," Logan calls from the adjoining room, "you're going to turn into a mermaid."

I stare at the skin on my fingertips; indeed, it's already all wrinkled up. I don't care, though, I'm not getting out of this tub for anything in the world.

"I've ordered dinner," Logan says.

I don't reply.

"Burgers and champagne."

Okay, now he's got my attention.

"And I've planned something special for dessert."

"What?" I call back.

"I can't tell you unless you come out and see for yourself."

"Sorry," I say. "This bath is too good."

"Are you sure? Because dessert involves chocolate-covered strawberries hand-fed to you while naked in bed."

Burgers, champagne, and a naked handfeeding of chocolate strawberries?

No bath is that good.

I pull the tub stopper with my toes and get up as the water swirls down the drain. I use the showerhead to rinse my body of all the remaining foam and then step out of the tub, wrapping myself in a fluffy white towel.

Hot water, clean towels, food. Things I'm never again taking for granted.

In the bedroom, Logan isn't much more dressed than me. He's sitting at the small, round table wearing only his boxer briefs. His chest, arms, and legs are covered in bruises and bug bites. And his knees are still swollen from the impact with the ravine. Both our bodies have seen better times. But... mostly naked Logan? Another thing I'll never take for granted.

I scowl. "I thought you promised me a naked dinner?"

"Naked dessert," he corrects. "You must endure clothes for the burgers and champagne."

I sigh theatrically. "The hardships you put me through."

We ravage the food with the enthusiasm of two people who've recently spent seventy-two hours eating basically nothing. And dessert turns out to be as worthy of an abandoned bath as Logan had promised. We make love well into the night and fall asleep curled in each other's arms.

Who would've guessed the standoffish Dr. Logan Spencer was a cuddler?

* * *

We spend the next week suspended in this beautiful limbo where we live together in a hotel room, make love as we wake up, eat a lush breakfast, and take a cab to the hospital to visit Archie.

The rest of the day Logan passes at the Thai Fine Arts Department, while I settle in a nearby cafe working on my computer to post-produce all the photos I took in the jungle. We eat lunch together, work more in the afternoon, pay Archie another visit, and then we go back to the hotel for another night of passionate lovemaking.

It'd be a perfect life, if not for the ticking timer attached to it.

Archie will be discharged from the hospital in two days. He and Logan have already booked a flight to San Francisco. Archie, to take some well-deserved downtime. Logan, to give his dean and the college foundation sponsoring the expedition a full report on our discovery. He needs to ask for more funds before he flies back to Trat to supervise the cataloging of all the treasures we uncovered and study the civilization that lived in the lost city. With a site so vast and untouched, the process will take months. Logan will have to move to Thailand.

I, too, have booked a flight home to LA. A near-death experience has been enough to make me reevaluate a few of my life's choices. Like the one of not talking to my sister over a boy scuffle. First thing I'll do when I get home is bang on her door and hold Summer in my arms so tightly, she'll beg me to let go. Then we'll crawl into her California king bed and stay awake all night talking until we fall asleep, like we used to do when we were kids.

The only remaining question is: with our lives moving in such opposite directions, what's going to happen to Logan and me?

* * *

Logan

. . .

"Man," Archie says, packing the last of his clothes in his rucksack. We're in his hospital room, and I'm helping him get ready for the long flight home. Winter has gone to the cafeteria for a coffee run. From here, the three of us will share a cab straight to the airport. "Please tell me the photographer owes me 200 bucks, yeah?"

"What are you talking about?"

"Back at camp, I bet her 100 dollars you'd screw each other's brains out before the expedition ended." Archie folds a shirt on the bed and then turns his piercing blue gaze on me. "She raised me 200 you guys wouldn't."

The statement takes me aback.

Without having specifically agreed on it, both Winter and I have been very discreet with PDAs in front of our friends. No real reason why, I guess we just wanted to enjoy the privacy of our new relationship. But Archie knows me too well...

From the mischievous twinkle in his eyes, I can tell he'll tease me until the end of time.

"Don't even try to deny it, man," he adds.

"Okay, I won't."

He pats me on the shoulder, affectionately but mockingly. "My boy, you make your old man proud."

I push his hand away. "Oh, stop it!"

"I'm sorry." Archie laughs. "But Dr. Logan Spencer breaking his own rules—to never mix business and pleasure—and for a woman! Not an everyday sight. But, heck, I've met the lady... so I understand, buddy, and I forgive you."

"Forgive me for what?"

"For placing yourself before the mission..." With pretend gravity, he repeats back to me all the warnings about dating a colleague I'd given him weeks ago at the resort. "For risking the expedition on a skirt and a pair of legs, for—"

"Okay, okay, I get it," I interrupt. "The moral high ground is yours."

Archie throws his last T-shirt into the rucksack and ties the cover, then, turning to me, he asks, "So is it just sex, or"—he cups his hands under his chin and, eyes exasperatingly wide, bats his eyelashes—"are there feelings involved?"

A knock on the door prevents me from answering.

"Is everyone decent?" Winter asks from the other side.

Archie answers first. "Nothing you haven't seen before, Snowflake." Then he looks at me in a you're-not-off-the-hook way. His unanswered question hangs in the air between us.

Winter comes in and gives me a paper coffee cup. Instinctively, I wrap an arm around her waist and stamp a kiss on her full lips.

Startled blue eyes stare up at me.

"We're busted," I explain. "He knows."

Winter turns to Archie, smiles, and shakes her head. "Oh, we're never going to hear the end of it, are we?"

If Archie's devilish grin is any indication, no, we're not.

Winter hands Archie his coffee, then takes a sip from her cup. "Can you at least wait until I'm properly caffeinated before unloading the heavy artillery?"

Archie gives a magnanimous nod. "Sure, Snowflake." And, with a teasing grin, he adds, "I'll think of all the things I can blow 200 bucks on in the meantime."

She rolls her eyes, but with a smile, and changes the subject. "Are we good to go?"

"Yes," I say.

"Actually," Archie says, "would you mind waiting for us downstairs?"

Winter raises her brows at him in a silent question.

"One bandage is hitching," he explains. "I'd like my boy here to take a quick look."

It sounds like an excuse, and from the small frown on Winter's face, I know she's thinking the same. But she doesn't question it. She shrugs in a boys-will-be-boys way, pulls on her rucksack, and with her coffee-free hand grabs the suitcase of city clothes she used to torture me with at the resort. But I can't blame her; I was an ass back then and deserved being messed with.

I hold the door open for her.

"Don't be too long," she says. "Traffic can be unpredictable in Bangkok, and we already don't have much of a cushion."

I nod and give her a quick kiss on the forehead.

When she's gone, I turn to Archie. "What is it?"

He stands leaning against the wall, arms crossed over his chest, studying me. "You haven't answered my question."

"What question?"

"Are you in love with her?"

Ah.

"Why do you ask?"

"To know what you plan to do here, man."

I gape in shock for a moment. "Are you seriously lecturing me on how to behave with women? You?"

"Well, this is the first woman I owe my ass to, and twice over, so I've grown pretty fond of her."

"Then you don't have to worry. My intentions are nothing but honorable."

Archie doesn't look convinced. "So you've already had the talk?"

"What talk?"

"Buddy, I'm not sure if you've noticed, but in three hours"—

he taps his watch for emphasis—"you're on a flight to San Francisco and she's heading back to LA. Have you guys discussed the logistics of the long-distance relationship scenario?"

"No, but we're cool. Winter is cool. We haven't figured out the details yet, but—"

"Have you talked about it, like, at all?"

"Not exactly. But—"

"And she's okay with it?"

"She must be; she hasn't brought the topic up once."

"And why haven't you?"

"I don't know, it didn't come up." Enough with the grilling. "Would you back off on the third degree and chill?"

"Yeah, man, all right. Just one last piece of advice..."

"Yeah?"

"If you love her... tell her before she boards that plane."

* * *

The discussion with Archie leaves me pensive. The slight tension between us lingers in the confined cab ride to the airport. So we don't talk. I'm too busy introspecting.

Am I falling short with Winter? Does she expect some grand gesture or something from me? How are we going to say goodbye? My original plan was to surprise her in LA as soon as I was done giving my reports to the university and foundation boards, so I've kept my intentions quiet. Has she taken my silence as a sign that I don't care? Surely not. She must know I'm serious about us.

She must.

Winter, too, is quiet. She seems to be lost in her own thoughts, staring out the window at the Bangkok skyline with a faraway look, like she's not taking in anything she's seeing.

Mmm. Maybe Archie had a point.

The silent ride to Suvarnabhumi Airport takes slightly over an hour, and, as Winter predicted, we're tight for time, especially her, since her flight leaves forty-five minutes earlier than ours.

All business-like, the three of us enter the airport and split right away to drop off our luggage at our respective check-in booths. The lines are similar in length, and we all get our boarding passes at the same time.

We regroup shortly afterward in front of the security check gates.

Winter looks up at me with a strained smile. "So I guess this is goodbye," she says. "I should be hurrying; my plane will start boarding soon."

Tension marks her features, and, with Archie's warning ringing loud and clear in my ears, I begin to wonder if I should really tell her I love her.

But here? At the airport? While we're pressed for time and about to leave... seems highly unromantic...

Still, now I'm nervous. Archie is doing his best to be inconspicuous. He would've probably left us alone already, if his abrupt departure wouldn't make this even more awkward. And Winter... she's still looking at me with those impossibly big blue eyes.

What do I do now?

I let out a nervous laugh. "So, I just figured I don't even have your phone number..."

"My phone number?" Winter spits out.

I know that pout. It promises nothing good.

"Yeah, you know, to keep in touch."

Her eyes narrow, and she looks more like the Winter of the first days we met. The woman giving me grief about almost everything and not the warm, loving creature of the past week.

Boarding pass and passport in one hand, she takes a step toward me. "You want to keep in touch?" The question comes out in a hiss.

"Yeah?"

What am I doing wrong here?

"I'll tell you what," she snaps. "Why don't you friend me on fucking Facebook, then!"

And with that, she spins on her heel, walks toward the security gate checkpoint and, showing her boarding pass to the officer at the head of the line, marches away on the other side.

I'm already running after her. "Winter, wait!" I call.

When I reach the officer, I hand him my ticket. But after one quick look at the papers, the attendant shakes his head at me. "This is fast track only." He points at the sign above the queuing lane entrance.

"Well, I don't have a fast-track pass," I say in a panic. "But I need to reach that woman."

"Sorry," the man says. "This line is only for passengers with a fast-track ticket."

"Winter!" I call again. I can still see her on the other side as she removes her jacket and places her bag in a plastic box to feed it through the baggage scanner. "Winter, wait! Winter!"

She doesn't hear me—or, pretends not to. And then she's past the metal detector and walking away. Away from me. Away from us.

I stare to my left at the regular security line, and my shoulders sag in defeat. The queue is too long. I'll never catch up with her before she boards her flight.

"I'm sorry, sir," the officer says. "If you don't have a fast-track pass, I need you to move aside."

A heavy arm drops on my shoulders and steers me away.

Archie gives me a pat on the chest with his other hand. "Attaboy; that went well... eh?"

* * *

Winter

Did I overreact?

I spend the journey home asking myself that question over and over again.

Unfortunately, I have a disproportionate amount of time to obsess. The itinerary back to California is crap. Some volcano in the Philippines decided to throw a little cinder and sparks party over the weekend, making the shortest, east-bound route to LAX closed off to all flights. So I'm rerouted to London Heathrow first, then New York JFK, and finally LAX.

A nightmare of a trip for every traveler, but for one journeying with a broken heart, like yours truly, it's unbearable.

So, did I overreact?

I'm not sure what exactly Logan said that set me off like that. I know I can be impulsive. But where I spent our time in Bangkok trying to figure out how we could make our relationship work—Should I move to Berkeley? Could he transfer to UCLA? Should we do long-distance for a while?—Logan, apparently, hadn't given it a second thought.

Maybe I'm the idiot for assuming we were on the same— serious relationship—page. But if he didn't quit his job for Tara after so many years together and with wedding bells on the horizon, he's not going to do it for me after a week of jungle romance.

The idiot asked for my phone number... to keep in touch.

What does that even mean?

The question tortures my poor brain hour after hour. On the first plane, I don't sleep. On the second, somewhere over the Atlantic, I pass out due to sheer exhaustion, but when we land in New York I'm none the more rested. I still feel like crap, have found no answers to my questions, and I'm dying for a decent, not-in-flight cup of coffee.

With a four-hour layover ahead of me, at least I have plenty of time to get a lavish breakfast.

Inside the airport, my gate hasn't been announced yet. So I wait in the general hub and stop at a nice bar with a clear view of the departures board. It's not exactly a coffee shop, but I like the look of their fancy Italian coffee maker and of the donuts on display over the counter. I need the caffeine, the sugar, and the saturated fats. This is my place.

"Hi." I sit at one of the high stools that line the main bar counter. "A cappuccino and a donut please."

"Single or double glaze?" the bartender—a friendly-looking guy with sandy hair and blue eyes—asks.

"Definitely double."

"On its way."

Five minutes later he places my breakfast in front of me. "Sugar's right there." He points at a glass jar on the counter.

"Thanks."

I add a sprinkle of sugar to my coffee and tuck in. At record speed, I consume everything, my stomach still grumbling once I'm done.

The bartender clears the empty plate and mug in front of me. "Can I get you anything else?"

"What other breakfast food do you have?" I could eat another donut, but now I'm craving something savory.

"We do paninis," the bartender says as if reading my mind. "Cheese and ham?"

"Yes, please. And an orange juice, please."

He nods, smiles, and gets to work making the sandwich and feeding oranges to the juicer machine.

"Here you go," he says, placing the food and drink in front of me.

I take a bite of toast and moan my appreciation. "Gosh, I really needed this."

"Long flight?" he asks.

"Long everything."

"Not a fan of plane food?"

"Who is?"

"No one, you're right."

The bartender lets me enjoy my second breakfast in peace, but when he comes to clear my plate again, he asks, "Traveling for business or pleasure?"

"Ah." I scoff. "Business; no pleasure whatsoever!"

"Oh, I'm sorry. Bad trip?"

"Bad boss."

"Ouch. What did he or she do?"

"He. At first, the idiot behaved like a jerk just because I'm a woman. Then, he made me fall in love with him. And when I was completely head over heels gone, what did the prick do?"

The bartender shrugs in a no-idea way.

"He went and asked for my phone number... to keep in touch! Bah! What does that even mean? What do you think he meant?"

"Err... I need more information to make a proper assessment. Like, how did he go from being a jerk to making you fall for him?"

And before I know it, I'm telling this guy the whole story.

From my first encounter with naked Logan, to the expedition in the jungle, the lost city, Smith and his rogue mercenaries, our escape, up until our wretched farewell at Bangkok airport yesterday.

When I finally shut up, the bartender lets out a low whistle. "Whoa, that's quite a story. In my job, I hear many tales... but this adventure... wow!"

Did I overshare? Maybe I overshared. But when I'm nervous, I talk. When I'm tired, I talk. When I'm both, I crash into TMI land like a cannonball.

"Sorry," I say. "I've unloaded my life story on you and haven't even introduced myself. I'm Winter Knowles."

"Mark Cooper," he says, and offers me his hand to shake.

Another customer sits a few stools away from me, and Mark goes to serve him before he comes back to me and begins unloading the bar dishwasher.

Eager to hear a second opinion, I ask, "So, what do you think Logan meant by asking for my number?"

"Honey, I really can't tell you if he's in love with you or not. But running away probably wasn't the best way to find out."

"I know, right?" I bite my lower lip. "But I had a plane to catch, and he just made me so mad."

"Or..." Mark stops sorting dishes and looks me straight in the eye. "You were afraid of the answer and preferred to bail before you found out."

"Oh, gosh." I cover my face with my hands and, peeking between my fingers, I say, "You might be right. So what do I do now?"

Mark gives me a warm smile. "You go home, get some rest, and then go get the man! He's coming back to the States, too, right?"

"Mm-hm. But shouldn't I wait for him to come to me?"

With a mock-serious raised brow, Mark asks, "Are you really into all that men-should-make-the-first-move crap?"

"No," I admit. "Not really."

"Then we have a plan!"

"You're right, thank you. Even if Logan says he doesn't want to be with me, I need to know either way."

"All passengers. Flight AA 171, with direct service to Los Angeles LAX, is beginning to board at gate 46. We're going to start boarding families with small kids and passengers with special needs. Then, we're going to board first and business-class passengers. And finally, all other passengers…"

"Oh, that's my flight!" I say, getting up. "How much do I owe you?"

Mark hands me the bill and takes my credit card. "You need your receipt?"

"No, thanks," I say. "Just a bit of luck."

Mark winks at me. "This Logan guy would be an idiot to let you go."

I nod, ready to head to my gate. "I agree with you. Let's hope he does, too."

22

LOGAN

Idiot. Jerk. Fool. Moron. Stupid. Imbecile. Heedless baboon...

After twenty hours in the air and a three-hour layover in Paris, I've run out of insults with which to call myself. I had the perfect woman, and I let her slip through my fingers.

"Man, enough already with the pity party," Archie says, cutting into my thoughts as we disembark at JFK. "Yeah, you've been a boneheaded monkey..." Boneheaded monkey! I'll add that to my list. "...but once we get back to Berkeley, LA will be only a short trip away. Fly down there and woo the lady all over again. If she fell for it once..."

We follow the directions toward our connecting flight, turning down a hall, then another, until we reach our terminal.

Archie bumps into me on purpose, prompting me to scold him. "Can you please be serious for once in your life?"

"Nah, you're grim enough for the both of us," Archie says, and points at a bar just below the departures board. "How about some overpriced Italian coffee?"

We sit at the counter, and I let him order for me as well. "One espresso for me, and a double for my friend."

The bartender nods and, with efficient, practiced motions that seem second nature to him, grinds the coffee beans, loads the black powder into the shiny coffee machine, and brews away.

He serves Archie first, and when he places my mug in front of me, he asks, "Need that extra kick, huh?"

The last thing I want is to discuss my problems with a total stranger, so I give him a noncommittal grunt in reply.

The guy seems to take the hint and walks away to busy himself with the drying of glasses or other bartender-y stuff. But Archie calls to him, "Excuse my friend, he's having a bit of a hard time."

"Bad work trip?" the bartender asks.

"No, man," Archie replies. "The other thing."

"Ah, a woman, then."

"What else?"

They share a knowing stare, half-serious, half-mocking, at my expense.

I scowl at Archie for spilling the beans about my private life, then drink my coffee in brooding silence. I won't be baited into talking.

"Ah," the guy behind the counter sighs. "All my patrons today seem to be suffering from woes of the heart."

"Really?" Archie asks.

Apparently, my friend is in a chatty mood. How fun for me.

"Yeah, a woman just left after telling me the most incredible story about naked archeologists, jungle treasure quests, ex-Special Forces gone rogue..."

My ears prickle at that, and suddenly all the exhaustion of the long journey evaporates out of me, steamed out by the bartender's words.

"Was she tall, with white-blonde hair?" I interrupt. "The woman?"

"Yeah, why? Oh my gosh." His eyes widen as he stares at me. "You're Logan!"

I jump off the stool with such force I send it tumbling to the floor. "How long ago did she leave?"

The bartender checks his watch. "Not twenty minutes ago, man; you should be able to catch her if you run."

"You know what flight she was on?"

"American Airlines, I think." He glances up at the departures screen. "They've just started boarding."

I follow his gaze to the big board with all the flights listed in orderly rows, scanning furiously for Winter's flight. There! American Airlines to LAX, gate 46.

"Thank you, man," I say, already taking my first step backward. If I had the time, I'd jump behind the bar and kiss the guy. But I don't have a second to spare. I won't screw this up again. "Archie, can you—"

"I've got it covered, Logie Bear," he says. "Go!"

"Thank you," I say.

As I turn and run, Archie calls after me, "And try not to screw it up this time!"

I race through the concourse like I'm twenty years old again and playing football. The drive is on, the end zone, gate 46. The gate gallery is my open field. I break into it, dodging travelers with luggage in tow, toddlers escaping their mothers, airport electric carts... I scamper yard after yard, the ball is my heart, winning Winter back will be my touchdown.

I look up at the gate signs, numbers flying by.

Gate 25. I'm halfway there!

The momentary distraction almost makes me crash into a family of four assembled outside a newswire, but at the last second, I skim left and avoid smashing the teenage son to the ground by a hairbreadth.

I run on.

Gate 31.

Gate 37.

While I run, I scan the crowds for a white-blonde head.

By gate 42, I'm winded hard. I'm really not twenty years old anymore. But I summon the last dregs of energy and force my legs to pump forward.

When I finally reach gate 46, there's a long line of passengers waiting to board the plane. The flight attendants are already letting people in.

Panic strikes.

Panting hard, I search the queue for Winter while my pulse speeds out of control, both from the physical effort and the fear that I've missed her again.

But then her unmistakable blonde hair waves at me like a signal flag in between two tall, athletic types, who, judging from the breadth of their shoulders, could be real NFL players.

"Winter," I call. But the sound comes out half-strangled and not nearly loud enough for her to hear me.

Hands on my knees, I take a few deep breaths until my respiration goes back to almost normal.

"Winter," I shout again. "Winter, wait!"

I walk up the line until I'm right beside where she's standing.

"Winter!"

Her head finally turns, and her eyes go wide as they meet mine.

23

WINTER

Fatigue has officially fried my brain, because I'm hallucinating. I see Logan standing next to me in the boarding queue. But that's impossible.

"Winter, wait... Don't get on the plane," phantom Logan pants, visibly out of breath. "I have to talk to you."

Only his voice sounds real, and he looks real, and other people are staring at him, too, so... he must be real!

I gently push past the two hunks behind me and exit the boarding line. "Logan? Where did you come from?"

He bends over slightly, still panting. "Bar... Other side of the airport." He points backward. "Dude behind the counter said you'd just left..."

"Mark?"

Logan nods. "Made a run for it on no sleep, no food, but I had an espresso so I guess I'm okay."

He's finally stopped panting, but, curiously enough, now I feel out of breath.

I take a step toward him. "Why?"

"To say what I should've told you in Bangkok."

I wait for him to elaborate. Let's see if this time he can come up with something better than, "Let's keep in touch."

"Being with you," Logan starts without preamble, "is like playing football—and not just because I had to make a drive through half of JFK to get to you. When I'm with you I feel like I felt in the tunnel before a game, waiting to run out on the field... so nervous and scared I wanted to puke..."

I startle at that. "You're saying I make you want to vomit?"

"Yes, but in a good way."

A man in the crowd calls, "Let the man say his piece!"

I glare at the audience, trying to scare the busybody into silence and then turn back to Logan.

"The wait in the tunnel is dark," he continues, and I really hope he has a point, because so far this isn't going any better than the I-don't-have-your-phone-number debacle. But I keep my mouth shut and, as the kind spectator suggested, let him say his piece. "You can hear the crowd buzzing outside, shouting, the commentators making their pre-game remarks while you wait, and the tension mounts and mounts. Then the speaker calls your team, and suddenly you're running into the light with the boom of 60,000 people cheering you on and butterflies exploding in your stomach. It's an exhilaration like nothing else I've ever felt in my life... until I met you."

There's a general "aww" from the crowd, who apparently find us more interesting than, you know, boarding the plane that's about to leave. Even the gate attendants are staring.

A little air pocket bursts in my stomach, as if the ground has just disappeared from beneath my feet. I can see now why the tunnel analogy is a good one.

But Logan isn't finished. "Yesterday," he continues, "thinking I'd lost you... it was like being trapped in the tunnel forever...

because being in love with you has been the best run into the light of my life."

There they are. Those words I was dying to hear and was starting to fear would never pass his lips. I smile as tears of joy stream down my cheeks. I close the distance between us and push a strand of hair behind Logan's ear. "You're in love with me?" I ask.

"Yeah." He scratches the back of his head, looking sheepish. "Guess I should've just come out with it and told you yesterday."

"Yep." I nod. "You really should have. Good thing I'm a very understanding woman..." Then I grab him by the collar of his shirt and pull him down into a kiss.

And we could really be in a stadium, because everyone around us starts clapping and cheering.

Self-consciously, I break the kiss and hide my face against Logan's chest.

"Attention, passengers," one of the gate attendants says over the boarding booth's speaker system. "As much as we all love a little airport romance, I still have to ask you to continue the boarding process so that we can ensure a timely departure for our flight."

The cheering stops, and all my fellow passengers get back in line to have their passports and boarding passes checked.

"Don't leave," Logan pleads. "Come to San Francisco with me!"

I wish I could... but... "I can't," I say. "There's someone I need to see at home."

Logan frowns.

"My sister," I explain. "I want to tell Summer I forgive her."

Logan nods. "Okay. I'd come to LA with you, but work... I have to..."

"I know, don't worry." I let him off the hook.

"But as soon as I've given my reports," Logan continues, "I'll hop on a plane and meet you in LA."

A pang of fear pulls at my chest. "And then what?" I ask. "How are we going to make this work?"

"Our jobs are flexible," Logan says. "I can be in LA when I don't have lectures—I only teach one semester a year—and you can be in Berkeley when I do... And we can try to make our work trips coincide. And when we can't manage that, well, those months will suck, but we could..." He pauses for a second. "I don't know... talk over the phone?" He flashes me a playful grin. "Assuming you'll ever give me your number."

I smile at that and kiss the man again. He can have my number, he can have my heart, he can have my everything...

"Attention, passengers, this is the last call for American Airlines flight 171 with direct service to LAX. Boarding will close in five minutes."

Reluctantly, I pull away from Logan. I'm the only passenger left at the gate.

"I have to go," I say.

Logan pushes a lock of hair away from my face, saying, "All right," and then kisses me on the forehead.

He walks me to the entrance and waits with me while the flight attendant scans my boarding pass and checks my passport. Then it's really time to say goodbye.

Logan cups my face, giving me a gentle kiss on the lips. "I'll see you soon."

I rise on my toes so I can whisper in his ear, "I love you, too, by the way."

And before I change my mind, I turn and run down the tunnel onto the plane, ready to fly home. Eager to make peace with my sister, and then be free to embark on the biggest adventure of my life yet... loving Logan and being loved by him.

* * *

Turns out I don't need to go to my sister's apartment and bang on her door to tell her I forgive her. The moment I step out of baggage claim at LAX, I spot her and Lana on the other side holding between them a gigantic cardboard that reads "Lara Croft". They've even sketched a liking of Lara next to the name. In the drawing, the video-game icon is staring fiercely out from the cardboard. Guns ablaze, signature shorts and teal tank top on, long braid reaching to her waist. The only difference to the real one is the hair color that they've turned blonde to resemble me.

Luggage in tow, I run toward them. They run toward me, and we collide midway. I drop my rucksack on the floor and pull them into a three-way hug. The setting of the reunion is not what I had imagined, but the hug is as tight. And Lana being here only makes it better. All three of us are laughing and crying and I don't even know why, but I know what I came home to say.

I pull back and stare my sister directly in the eyes. "I'm sorry for being a stubborn cow. I forgive you, fully, completely. Nothing you could do would make me love you any less. We're twins and you're stuck with me for life."

The quivering in Summer's lower lip worsens, and she covers her face with her hands. "No, I'm sorry. I ruined everything and for nothing."

Lana and I exchange a look and we both hug her.

"I don't deserve you," Summer bawls. "Neither of you."

It takes Lana and me a lot of whispered soothing words and reassuring gestures to convince Summer everything will be all right and make her stop crying.

I don't mind. I've missed my twin sister, and I'm only realizing how much now that she's holding me with the tenacity of a baby macaque.

Once she finally lets go, I suggest, "Why don't we go celebrate that I made it home in one piece at a fancy bar? Drinks are on me."

Summer shakes her head. "Sorry, I'm on strict orders to bring you straight home to Mom and Dad."

I frown. "To Pasadena?"

"Yep." She nods. "It's the least you can expect after having the embassy call them to say you'd been kidnaped by rough militia 13,000 miles from home. It's already a miracle I convinced them not to drive here in the middle of the night to pick you up."

Summer takes a hold of my trolley while Lana picks up my rucksack from the floor and loops it on her shoulder. "Come on," she says. "You're getting the VIP treatment. Christian's driver is taking us."

I drop one arm on each of their shoulders. "Uh, our very own celebrity chauffeur, I could get used to this."

And especially to our friendship being on the way to making a full comeback.

EPILOGUE
WINTER

Two months later

I'm back in Thailand. The Bangkok Museum of Art is about to inaugurate its most anticipated exposition ever—the unveiling of the ancient treasure we discovered in the lost city. No, I'm not visiting as a tourist. A certain broody archeology professor recommended me for the role of official photographer for the expo, meaning we've spent the past three weeks together in this beautiful country.

It hasn't been the most exciting work so far, as I've spent most days holed up in the museum's basement photographing every single archeological find that has been dug out of the lost city.

But at least no jungles this time, only five-star hotels and bubble baths for us. A short, idyllic break from reality.

I leave in a week for a new assignment in Cambodia, and I'd be lying if I said the sense of déjà vu at my imminent departure isn't strong.

Not complete déjà vu as Logan now tells me he loves me any chance he gets. It's the first thing he whispers in my ear as I open my eyes. He says it again when he holds me close at night. Or when we cross paths at the museum. He puts it at the end of every text exchange. Leaves it written in cheesy messages in the foggy mirror after a shower. But even if I'm sure of his feelings, long-distance relationships suck.

We had a taste of how much being apart blows when he had to fly back to Thailand a mere week after we'd reunited in the States. He surprised me in LA three days after his airport declaration, and we spent every waking hour together, kissing, talking, making love, and then, puff, he was up in a plane again headed here and I was stuck back home, fifteen time zones away.

And now, the prospect of me doing the same and packing up to go to Cambodia for two weeks is daunting. I used to love the idea of embarking on a new adventure, of traveling the world, but now all I crave is putting on a pair of slippers and spending a quiet night in with Logan by my side.

"You're not dressed."

The object of my fantasies yanks me out of my reverie, placing himself in front of me, hands on his hips, signature scowl on his face.

I used to find his constant frowning upsetting. Now it's one of the things I love to tease him about.

I bat my lashes at him from my position in front of the dresser where I got lost in thought, wearing only a towel. "I could argue you're too dressed."

His features immediately soften and he squats next to me. "And on any other day, I'd take you up on that offer."

My turn to frown. "Why not today?"

"Because we're going to be late."

"Late for what?"

Logan gives me a saucy grin. "Your private tour of the exhibition before the grand opening tomorrow."

I throw my hands in the air, standing up. "This is what I get for dating an archeology professor, someone who'd prefer going to a museum rather than having sex."

Logan stands up, a playful grin curling his lips, and pulls me in for a kiss. "You'll be glad you came, I promise, my love," he says, nuzzling my neck.

My skin sizzles under the gentle scrape of his stubble. "You're not making the argument of museum versus sex a strong one."

"Sorry." He pulls back and gives me a playful spank. "Go get dressed."

In a last-ditch attempt to provoke him, I let my towel drop.

The low growl I receive in response brings me great satisfaction. I saunter to the closet and pull on a cotton summer dress, peeking at Logan over my shoulder only when I'm fully covered again.

His gaze is fixed on me, predatory.

"I'm ready to go," I say, the image of innocence.

Logan pulls me into a passionate kiss and lets me go only when I've turned into a limp rag doll in his arms.

He winks and gives me a gentle push toward the door. "Let's go."

The museum is already closed to the public when we arrive. Logan uses his employee badge to let us in from a side entrance. From there, we hedge along a narrow corridor and then move one floor up to the main lobby where the new exhibition is situated.

Logan guides me with a hand on the small of my back that

does nothing to convince me I'd not rather be under the sheets in our hotel room now.

"Close your eyes," he bends to whisper in my ear.

A shiver runs down my spine. I comply with the request only to make the visit shorter so that I can bring him back to the hotel and finally have my way with him. The mental countdown to my departure has started in my head. We're at minus six nights before I leave, and I want to make the most of our time together.

With me blind, Logan has to guide me forward, gently steering me by the shoulders.

We stop as he pushes a door open, ordering, "Don't peek, not yet."

I make a show of squinting my entire face so as not to look.

With a chuckle, Logan leads me ahead. "All right, smartass, you can look now."

My jaw drops when I open my eyes.

I'm transported back into the cathedral-like atrium of the temple we entered in the lost city. But with better lighting. I stare stupefied at the twin rows of shiny pillars lining the room.

"Are these real?" I ask Logan, touching one.

"No, just a replication."

Under my fingertips, I recognize the feel of paper mâché, painted gold to shine.

"But the statues are real," Logan adds, giving a chin nod to the back of the room.

Garuda, the winged man, Yasha, the fierce warrior, and Mock, the monkey god of justice, greet me like old friends.

"You had them brought here all the way from the jungle?"

"It was quite a feat."

We walk over to the colossi. My first instinct would've been to touch the middle statue, but they're all picketed within a circle of red rope to prevent me and other tourists from doing just that.

"Why bring them to Bangkok?"

"The jungle site is too remote for most people to visit."

I scoff at that. "Yeah."

"The government has decided to make this a permanent expo and showcase as much of the treasure as possible."

"Is Buddha here, too?"

"Next room." Logan beckons me forward.

In the museum, we don't have to navigate a narrow, dark passageway to reach the reclining Buddha, just cross into the next room, which, once again, is an almost exact replica of the second chamber we discovered in the temple, down to the entrance to the secret passage and the slab of stone blocking it.

I laugh at that. "Don't tell me the patrons will have to search for the switch to move forward."

Logan grins. "Tour guides will show them the arcane, but we wanted to make the experience as realistic as possible."

With the enthusiasm of a kid let loose in Disney World, I press the carved disk identical to the one that lifted the stone door in the real temple. The faux stone slab rises in the same way, and we gain access to the treasure chamber.

The wooden boxes that used to contain the gold sit behind a protective glass display, even the one Smith mauled. A few coins are also displayed in a separate glass case. Similarly, the stone chests that held the diamonds and rubies are in their nook, empty of the gems. Only the pictures I took of the precious stones are exposed.

I'm about to ask where the gems will be kept when my attention is drawn to a waist-high column in the middle of the room covered by a square glass dome.

"What is this?" I peek inside to find a gorgeous gold ring with a blue stone set in its center.

Logan comes behind me, dropping his hands on my shoulders and his chin on the top of my head. "Do you like it? The blue reminded me of the color of your eyes."

"Yes, it's beautiful." I stare at the ring mesmerized, then frown. "Wait, I don't remember any jewelry from the temple? Did you find this somewhere else?"

Logan ignores my question and moves next to the display. "Would you like to try it on?"

He already has a hand on the glass, ready to lift it when I stop him. "Wait! Are you crazy? We can't touch museum property."

"This we can."

"Nope," I say. "I've seen this. I know how it unfolds. You'll trigger some kind of alarm and we'll get fried by red lasers."

While I check the ceiling to confirm laser guns are about to drop and be pointed at us, Logan takes advantage of my momentary distraction to retrieve the ring from under the protective case. I'm about to protest again when he drops to one knee.

Oh, gosh.

He clears his throat, and I yell, "Yes!"

Logan grins wide, shaking his head. "I had a speech ready, woman. At least let me give it to you."

I can't stop beaming at him. "Okay, but my answer will still be a sound yes."

Logan's face grows serious, his gaze tender. "Winter, in the short time I've known you, you've stolen my heart. You are the sun that lights up my day, the breeze that keeps me cool when the world is hot. You've been my strength when my own faltered." He takes my hand in his. "You're strong and fearless and you've been my safe place when everything was crumbling in on us. I know it sounds silly to ask you to marry me after only a couple of months, but to me, it doesn't feel like months. It feels like a lifetime, and I love you. I love all of you. You're my soul mate, my best friend, my everything. I want to spend my life with you. I want to share it, laugh with you, cry with you, and make a home with you. I love you, and I want to marry you."

He clears his throat again. "That was your cue to speak."

I just nod, because I can't speak. I'm too choked up. I drop to my knees in front of him and kiss his face, *everywhere*. I stamp a million kisses on his brows, his forehead, his cheeks, and finally, his mouth.

He's laughing when I stop at last. His arms circle around me, pulling me tight against him. I've never felt so safe, so secure, so complete.

My lips press against his, sharing his breath. "Yes."

I pull back, keeping my eyes on his. "I love you, Logan. And I want to marry you."

He takes hold of my hand and slips the beautiful ring on my finger.

Next thing I know, we're kissing and rolling on the floor of the museum until Logan regains his senses and pulls me up to sit.

"Err, there are no lasers, but I'm pretty sure they have cameras."

I laugh. "Oh, the security guard must be having a field day." My gaze drops to his kissed-out full lips. "Does your office have cameras, too?" I ask. I don't think I can wait until we make it back to the hotel.

With a feral grin, Logan says, "Nope." He springs upright and offers me a hand to pull me up.

Holding hands, we run across the fake temple chambers and the rest of the museum until we crash into his office.

I'm breathless when we arrive. Logan is too, but he doesn't waste a single moment to pull my dress over my head and toss it aside before he lays me on his desk and kisses me.

"I've wanted to do this since you put that stupid dress on."

I help him out of his shirt, giving him sexy eyes. "You could've just told me you wanted to skip hotel sex for naughtier museum sex."

Logan chuckles and slides his hand under my inner thigh, pulling me to him. He's slightly too enthusiastic and makes me lose my balance. To compensate, I lean into him too hard, positively toppling him over. We tumble to the floor in a mess of limbs and tangled, half-discarded clothes.

Half an hour later, we're still lying on the floor, with *no* clothes on, a blanket draped under and around us.

Still slightly out of breath, I stare at the ceiling and ask, "Should I worry you keep a sex blanket in the office?"

Logan guffaws. "Until today, that blanket has only been used for picnics when I took my lunch break outside, before this awful, never-ending rain started."

I roll to the side, propping my elbow up and resting my head on my hand. "Sorry I ruined your perfectly innocent blanket."

He grins and traces his fingertip down my cheek before dipping it under my chin to trace down my neck and collarbones. "I'll get another one." The touch of his finger against my skin is electric, and I shiver at the feel. I'll never get enough of this man.

Logan grabs my free hand, suddenly serious, kissing my knuckles and stopping to kiss our engagement ring. "There's something I wanted to talk to you about."

"Oh?"

"I know we said we'd adjust our relationship around our work schedules, but I no longer want to live in a different city from you. The moment I get back, I'm going to see if there are any openings in the history department at UCLA."

"You'd do that for me? Give up your job? You have tenure at Berkley."

"I'd go to the end of the world for you."

My heart swells with so much love I'm not sure it can be contained in my ribcage anymore. I brush a strand of hair away from his forehead. "You don't have to. Nothing is keeping me in LA; I'll move to The Bay Area."

"But your sister is there, your best friend. In San Francisco, you won't be as close to your family."

"You're going to be my family, and I've been in a long-distance relationship with everyone else in my life since I started traveling for my job. I know it works. What I can't bear is to be away from you. I hate that I have to leave for Cambodia in a week, and I'm not sure I want to keep that lifestyle in the future."

His thumb traces slow circles on my shoulders. "What are you saying?"

"That I might be in the market for a career change."

"And what would you do?"

"I taught a short photography course before coming to Thailand. I liked it."

"Really?" He sounds eager.

"Yes, why?"

Logan's finger travels leisurely down my arm and up again. "A friend told me there might be an opening at the Academy of Art University in San Francisco."

"Why didn't you tell me?"

"I didn't want to pressure you, or make it look like I was asking you to change for me, or giving more importance to my job over yours."

"Who are you and what have you done with my favorite, anti-feminist grump?"

The scowl promptly appears. "I've never been anti-feminist."

I kiss the frown away. "Should we call you slightly prejudiced then; you weren't exactly championing me when I joined your expedition."

His green eyes smolder, and he rolls half on top of me. "Only because I'd wanted to undress you from the moment I set eyes on you, and you were torturing me with those short shorts, scandalous bikinis, and braless black dresses."

I smirk, pleased with myself. "Oh, so you noticed."

"I noticed everything about you, from day one, from the small crease you get here in the middle of your forehead when you're displeased about something, down to the last freckle on your pretty nose." He presses his mouth to the part in question. When he pulls back up, he's looking all intense again.

"Uh-oh, your serious face is back."

"I just want to make sure you're not making rash decisions. That you're fine changing jobs."

"I am. I don't want to trot each month to a different continent and live out of hotel rooms. "

"I want to cut back on the traveling as well. I'll ask to teach more hours next year. The lost city was my life's work. I'm ready to settle. But are you sure you'll be fine just teaching?"

"I can still accept the odd assignment abroad if I get too restless, but make it the exception and not the norm. And as long as I don't have to turn into a wedding photographer, yeah, I'll be okay."

"Speaking of weddings... where do you want to host ours?"

"Home?"

"No exotic destination wedding?"

"Nah, we've had enough exotic for a while."

He taps my nose. "Most of my invitees will come from abroad. The celebrations need to be a longer-than-usual affair somewhere nice where people would want to visit."

"I'm okay with that. Any place you had in mind?"

"If you want to stay close to home, Big Sur and Napa are our best alternatives."

An image of endless, sunny vineyards pops into my head. "I like the sound of Napa."

Logan kisses my forehead. "Everything you want, my love."

"And Logan?"

"Yes?"

"Let's do it soon. I can't wait to become your wife."

AUTHOR'S NOTE

Dear Reader,

I hope you enjoyed reading *Love Quest*. If this is the first book in this series of interconnected rom-coms you've read, you can go back to *The Love Theorem* to meet Lana and her celebrity boyfriend Christian.

If you're an aficionado, thank you for following me on this entire journey. Now, I have a bit of an announcement. Sometimes, book characters can be really naughty and a certain sweet Viking, Mr. Archibald Hill, really snuck under my skin while I was writing this novel. I developed a writing crush on him and decided he deserved his own book. I also felt another one of my characters was being left a bit forsaken. So far, Summer Knowles, Winter's twin sister, has been the villain, the one we all hate. The cheater. The other woman. And, like Winter, it took me almost two novels to warm up to her again and even begin to consider she might deserve a happily ever after, too. So I thought to myself, mmm... what would happen if these two, Archie and Summer, were ever to meet? And—little spoiler—what better occasion for a meet-cute than Logan and Winter's wedding? So the idea for the next book in the series came along: *The Love Proposal*.

Now I have to ask you a favor. If you loved my story, please leave a review at your favorite retailer, Goodreads, or wherever you like to post reviews (your blog, your Facebook wall, your bedroom wall, a TikTok, in a text to your best friend...). Reviews are the best gift you can give to an author, and word of mouth is the most powerful means of book discovery.

I hope I haven't bored you too much with my babbling... Thank you for your constant support!

Camilla, x

ACKNOWLEDGMENTS

The first biggest thank you has to go to my best friend, Sara, who once told me a story about a gorgeous naked man yelling at a thieving monkey in a resort in Thailand. In the original story, Mr. Naked and Gorgeous exchanged his phone not for a banana but for a beer can that the monkey later enjoyed on the roof while still smashing the poor man's phone. Anyway, without this hilarious writing prompt, *Love Quest* wouldn't be here... so, many thanks.

Thank you to the amazing team at Boldwood Books for breathing new life into this story with an amazing makeover and for their awesomeness in general.

Thank you to my street team, and to all of you who leave book reviews. They're so important and appreciated.

Thank you to all my readers. Without your constant support, I wouldn't keep pushing through the blank pages.

Thank you to librarians for all the hard work they put into promoting the love of reading.

Thank you bookstagrammers and booktokers, I love seeing your beautiful pics and videos of my books. It's a thrill every time.

And lastly, thank you to my family and friends for your constant encouragement.

You're all heroes!

MORE FROM CAMILLA ISLEY

We hope you enjoyed reading *Love Quest*. If you did, please leave a review.

If you'd like to gift a copy, this book is also available as an ebook, hardback, large print, digital audio download and audiobook CD.

Sign up to Camilla Isley's mailing list for news, competitions and updates on future books.

https://bit.ly/CamillaIsleyNews

Discover fun-filled romantic comedies from Camilla Isley...

ABOUT THE AUTHOR

Camilla Isley is an engineer who left science behind to write
bestselling contemporary rom-coms set all around the world.
She lives in Italy.

Visit Camilla's website: https://camillaisley.com

Follow Camilla Isley on social media:

instagram.com/camillaisley

tiktok.com/@camilla.isley

facebook.com/camillaisley

twitter.com/camillaisley

bookbub.com/authors/camilla-isley

youtube.com/RomanceAudiobooks

Boldwood

Boldwood Books is an award-winning fiction publishing company seeking out the best stories from around the world.

Find out more at www.boldwoodbooks.com

Join our reader community for brilliant books, competitions and offers!

Follow us
@BoldwoodBooks
@BookandTonic

Sign up to our weekly deals newsletter

https://bit.ly/BoldwoodBNewsletter

Made in the USA
Las Vegas, NV
06 May 2024

89611990R00134